Countdown to Thanksgiving

Dianna Houx

Reading Order

1.) Countdown to Christmas
2.) Countdown to Valentine's Day
3.) Countdown to Easter
4.) Countdown to Mother's Day
5.) Countdown to 4th of July!
6.) Countdown to Halloween!
7.) Countdown to Thanksgiving!
8.) Countdown to Christmas Eve!
9.) Countdown to New Beginnings
10.) Countdown to a Wedding

I recommend reading the books in order. There is an overarching storyline that starts in book 1 and continues throughout the series. Plus, it's more fun that way!

Contents

Days till Thanksgiving

-Twelve-

How did the saying go: the best-laid plans of mice and men...yada yada yada. Grace couldn't remember, but it seemed appropriate given the circumstances. With a sigh, she shook her head and looked up at her boyfriend, no...fiancé, Cole. "Any chance it's not as bad as it looks?"

Cole winced, then stared back up at the tree, now leaning heavily against the roof of Grace's house. "It's possible," he said, though his tone conveyed his skepticism, "but it seems unlikely." He pulled her in front of him and pointed up toward the top of the house. "Do you see those boards sticking up through the branches?"

"Yes," she sighed again.

"Those are your rafters, darlin'." He put his arms around her waist and pulled her close. "I'm sorry, but at the very least, I think you're going to need a new roof."

Grace angled her face to look at him. "At the least?" she asked, her brow raised. "What would be the most?"

He didn't answer right away, which only served to make her more nervous. When Cole chose to remain silent, that usually meant he was trying to come up with a way to soften the news he was about to give her.

"Just tell me," she prodded him, "I'm not sure it can get much worse than this."

"How about, instead of speculating, we call the insurance company and let them handle this, okay?"

That seemed reasonable, so she decided not to argue. Instead, she followed him inside to talk to Granny, who they found sitting around the dining room table with Gladys, Grant, Molly, and baby Eliza.

"Two things," Molly said in her no-nonsense business tone. "One, Granny has just informed us that you do not have insurance on the house," she held up her palm to stop Grace from interrupting, "two, we have received a request from a family to host a Thanksgiving Experience, which could help solve problem number one."

If Cole hadn't wrapped his arms around her, Grace was certain she would have fallen backward in shock. Of all the times to find out they didn't have insurance, this was definitely the worst. Not to mention they'd hosted dozens of people over the last year without any sort of contingency against damages to or from the guests. They'd been on the brink of ruin so many times and hadn't even known it. She thought back to the antics between Valerie and Journey last Mother's Day and cringed. Either one of those women could have sued her, and there would have been nothing she could have done about it. Thankfully, that thought had never crossed Valerie's mind.

"Can I ask what happened to the insurance?" asked Cole.

Grace didn't have to look to know the muscle in his jaw was ticking. She could imagine the thoughts going through his mind, none of them good. Cole didn't know how bad things had been last Christmas. In all the time they'd been together, she had never told him how dire their situation had gotten, which in hindsight, was a huge mistake.

"I couldn't afford to pay it," said Granny, her voice quivering. "I'm so sorry." She said, her head hung in shame.

Molly reached over and placed her hand on top of Granny's. "This is partially our fault, too," she said gently. "Grant and I should have taken care of this when we took over managing the B&B's finances. I don't know what happened," she shook her head, "I guess we were all so busy it fell through the cracks."

"It's okay," echoed Cole. "I have a contractor buddy I can call. I'm sure he'll be willing to work with us. In the meantime, I think it's best if you guys stay elsewhere until the repairs have been made."

"We can stay at the hotel," said Grace. "That will be more convenient if I'm going to host a Thanksgiving Experience." She turned to Molly. "Do you think the family will mind staying at the hotel instead of here at the B&B?"

Baby Eliza began to fuss, and Molly picked her up out of her car seat and rocked back and forth with her. When she calmed back down, Molly replied, "I don't see why not. I will discuss it with them first, just in case." She looked down at Eliza for a moment and then back up at Grace.

"Are you sure about this, Grace? I know you need the money, but I also know you were looking forward to a family-only holiday."

"There is money in the emergency account," Grant interjected. "I don't know if it's enough to cover the damage, but it should be enough to get started."

Grace took a deep breath and then let it out slowly. She had been looking forward to a stress-free holiday; well, a less stressful holiday. This past year had been a lot of fun. After growing up an only child and spending all her holidays with just her granny, it had been nice to have a house full of guests to celebrate with. But having one holiday where she didn't have to worry about entertaining people for days on end would have been nice. Oh well, some other time.

"It's fine, guys, we can do the Experience. We only have twelve days until Thanksgiving. The rest of the town is still recovering from the storm, and Jilly and the kids are visiting her in-laws, but I'm sure we can work something out. When did the guests plan to arrive?" Grace asked, almost afraid to hear the response.

"Next Saturday," replied Molly. "That gives us a week to prepare. Is that enough time?"

"It's more time than I've had in the past," Grace teased, referring to Mother's Day when Molly accidentally booked the guests an entire week early.

Molly groaned. "Don't remind me, I still feel bad about that little mishap!"

Eliza began to fuss again, so Grant and Molly excused themselves to take her back home.

"I'll help Josie pack some of her things," said Gladys. She helped Granny to her feet, then grabbed her cane and followed her out of the room. "How long should we pack for?" she asked when they got to the door.

"At least a week," replied Cole. "But don't worry too much, Grace will still be able to come and get more clothing when needed."

Gladys nodded and continued to Granny's room, leaving Grace and Cole alone in the dining room.

"Where's Rebekah?" asked Cole.

"I'm not sure," replied Grace. "She went out sometime last night to help Thorne make some house calls, and I haven't seen her since."

"Good, I'd like to talk to you alone for once," he said, grabbing her hand and leading her into the foyer so they were less likely to be overheard. "I'd like you and Granny to stay with me at the farm. If you're willing, that is."

Grace's eyes widened in surprise. "Are you sure?"

Cole nodded. "I know we haven't made plans for where we'll live once we're married, but I feel like this would be a good trial run. Plus, Max would love to have Ruby and Piper to play with. Do you think Granny will agree?"

"I don't know," Grace drawled. "She's pretty old-fashioned."

"You can each have your own room," he assured her. "I'll even get Riley to come over and help me move Granny's bed into one of the spare rooms to make it easier on her. Deal?"

"Deal, but Cole, is there something else going on? This feels...I don't know, like you're being protective or something."

He glanced up at the tree, visible through the glass transom above the front door. "Do you see which part of the house the tree is sitting on?"

"Yes," she replied.

"And whose room is right beneath that tree?"

"Well, mine, but—

Cole pulled her close and wrapped his arms around her. "But, nothing. I could have lost you, Grace. I'd just feel better if you were close; that's all."

"I'm not in any danger at the hotel," she reminded him. "But I would love to stay with you, so I'll take the excuse."

"Thank you," he chuckled against her hair. "Why don't you pack while I call Riley and that buddy I mentioned? With any luck, we can have Granny settled into her new room by lunchtime."

"Sounds good." She stood on her tiptoes and gave him a quick kiss. "Thanks, Cole, I honestly don't know what I'd do without you."

He kissed her back, long and hard. "You'd figure it out, darlin', but I'm always happy to help." He kissed her one more time, then stepped out onto the porch to make his calls.

Grace watched him leave, then hurried upstairs to pack. She was looking forward to this much more than she should be considering the amount of damage to her house. But every tragedy was supposed to have a silver lining; she supposed this was hers. There was just one last detail to oversee: Rebekah.

***

Grace was loading bags into her car when Rebekah pulled up. She looked exhausted yet excited, the way one might look if they'd survived the night on coffee alone. "How'd it go?" she called out as Rebekah approached.

"Pretty well," she replied, her eyes glued to the tree. "Looks like you can't say the same."

"Cole's got a buddy on the way," Grace informed her. "We don't have insurance, Molly booked a family for a Thanksgiving Experience, and Jilly is out of town. How about you? Any news?"

Rebekah continued to stare at the tree. "You could have been killed."

"That seems to be the consensus." She shoved the rest of the bags into the trunk, then slammed it shut. Between her and Granny, it looked like they'd packed for a month. Grace couldn't remember the last time they'd been away from home like this. "So what'd you do last night?"

"Played mid-wife to a horse," she said, finally looking at Grace. "One of Thorne's patients began to foal in the middle of the storm and freaked out, so I went and tried to help keep her calm."

"Wouldn't that have been a better job for the owner?" Grace asked. "No offense," she hurried to add. "I'm sure you did a great job."

She shrugged, weariness showing in her expression. "The owners had their hands full with the storm. A tree fell onto a section of fence, and they had to repair it before their cattle got out." She shook her head. "I can't imagine trying to repair a fence in the middle of that wind and rain. It must have been awful."

"Can't say I disagree. Cole doesn't think staying here while they work on the house is safe, so Granny and I plan to stay with him out at the farm. Would you like to join us?"

Rebekah raised a brow. "Is there even room for me? I've only been in the house a couple of times, and it didn't seem that big."

"We would have to share a room, but it could be fun!" Grace said enthusiastically. "It'll be like Summer camp or whatever."

"Did you not have sleepovers when you were young?"

"No," Grace looked down in embarrassment. "I was the shy kid who struggled to make friends, remember?"

"Alright, fair enough. If we end up needing more space, I can always stay at the hotel."

Grace looked at her in horror. "By yourself?"

A smile formed on Rebekah's lips, followed by a chuckle that quickly turned into hysterical laughter. "You should see the look on your face," she choked out between laughs. "The hotel isn't really haunted, silly."

"I know, it's just, I've never spent the night alone before. It seems…I don't know, lonely. And even though that place isn't haunted, it still sounds like it is in the dark of the night."

Rebekah laughed again. "Listen to yourself; you sound all Edgar Allan Poe-ish. Regardless, I'm sure it will be fine. I won't be surprised if I end up with the bed all to myself anyway if you know what I mean," she said, elbowing Grace in the ribs.

"Whatever." Grace rolled her eyes. "Just go pack your things before you pass out from exhaustion."

"It was worth it," she called over her shoulder. "If this wedding planner business doesn't work out, I'm going to become a midwife.

"To humans or horses?" Grace teased.

"Horses," she replied, "definitely horses!"

Days till Thanksgiving

<h1 style="text-align: center;">-Eleven-</h1>

Waking up at the farmhouse had been a bit disorienting. Not because Grace wasn't used to it but because she wasn't used to doing it with a full house. Cole's place had always felt like a getaway, somewhere they could go to be alone. Now, with Rebekah, Granny, and all the pets, that feeling was gone, and she wasn't sure how to feel about it.

Things got even more chaotic when Gladys, Molly, Grant, and Eliza showed up just before she was about to start breakfast. Thankfully, they came bearing breakfast because Grace was unsure how she would have cooked for that many in Cole's tiny kitchen. And unlike Granny's dining table, which could seat twenty, Cole's...well, let's just say it did not seat twenty. Grace was not surprised to see Cole quickly disappear to the field, nor was she surprised when Max and Ruby followed. Piper, bless her, was more than happy to stick around and lap up as much attention as possible in the crowded space.

"So," Grace began once the food had been served, "what can you tell me about our soon-to-be new guests?"

They were spread out in the living room, a cozy fire going in the fireplace. Cole typically refrained from using the fireplace unless it was either frigid outside or they were having a date night, so she briefly wondered if he had imagined a much different start to their day than the one they got.

"Well," Molly said between bites, "the family is from Scotland. Or, they've been living in Scotland for a while; she wasn't clear in her email. Anyway, her name is Maisey, and she wants to bring her family over for an authentic American Thanksgiving meal."

Rebekah and Grace exchanged a look. "She's from Scotland?" Rebekah asked, a tinge of skepticism in her voice. "How did a woman from Scotland hear about a little B&B, in a little town, in rural Missouri?"

Molly's brow furrowed as she studied Grace and Rebekah. "She said she's a fan of Rebekah's and heard about us on social media. Why? Is there something I'm missing?"

Rebekah and Grace exchanged another glance. "Last we heard, Hunter is in Scotland," Rebekah explained. "And it seems like quite the coincidence that a family from Scotland wants to stay here, that's all."

It took a moment for Molly to process that, and when she had, she turned to Grant. "Anything you want to say to that?"

"Nope." Grant shook his head. "Hunter and I parted ways months ago. I have no idea where he is or what he's doing. While I agree this is a coincidence, it seems unfathomable to me that Hunter would agree to bring his girlfriend here, of all places."

"I agree that it doesn't make sense, but Hunter's done a lot of things that don't make sense. Would this really be that surprising?" asked Grace. "I mean, really, we're talking about a man who brought his girlfriend to my house without warning last Valentine's Day. This doesn't feel that out of character for him."

"To be fair, I did follow him," Rebekah pointed out. "But if you had known about me in the first place, none of that would have happened."

Gladys, who, to that point, had been silently observing, cleared her throat. "We can sit here and speculate till the cows home, my dears, but, in my opinion, only one course of action is available: to move forward as planned. If Hunter does end up involved, and that's a big if, then let the chips fall where they may."

"I agree," said Granny. "If we're going to take these people's money, then our focus needs to be on providing the best Experience we can for them."

Grace didn't want to agree, but she knew Granny was right. Her mission had always been to be the best host she could be, and this time was no different. Even if it turns out that Hunter is one of the guests. "Okay," she said, pasting a smile on her face, "we have a little less than a week to prepare. We need to clean the hotel, plan a menu, and come up with a list of activities to entertain the guests while they're here. Any ideas?"

"I can help clean the hotel," Rebekah volunteered. "I can also help with the menu."

"I'm sure Kenzie and Wyatt would be happy to host another wine tasting," said Molly. "Those seem to be popular with guests."

Rebekah nodded. "I can arrange that when I see Kenzie tomorrow. If they're going to arrive on Saturday, and leave the following Saturday, we really only need plans for six days. Five, if we consider the meal on Thanksgiving as the activity for that day."

"So if we go with the wine tasting, that means we only need four more activities," said Grace. "That seems a little less daunting."

"Keep in mind they're coming here for an American experience," Gladys reminded them. "The activities need to represent that."

Grant picked up the newspaper and opened it to the sports page. "I'll see if there's any football games scheduled for next week. There's nothing more American than football."

"We should meet with the town council and see if they have any ideas," said Grace. "It's possible some of them might want to get involved, and I don't want them to feel left out."

"You mean you don't want to miss out on an opportunity to foist your hosting duties on them," Rebekah teased.

Grace shrugged. "You're not wrong. Christmas was so much easier to plan. There are tons of activities for Christmas, not so much for the rest of the holidays. Each one seems to get more challenging than the last."

"Which reminds me," said Molly, "I'll rent a bus to chauffeur the guests like we did on Mother's Day. That seemed to work well and will make planning activities in other towns easier."

Grant folded the newspaper and laid it back down on the table. "There's a game on Monday. If Molly is able to book the tickets, I'll personally escort everyone there." He leaned over to kiss Molly and Eliza on the cheek and stood. "Unfortunately, I need to go to work. Good luck, guys!"

"What a way to take one for the team," Molly said with a laugh. "I'll book the tickets today, which brings us down to three."

"I'm fresh out of ideas, so let's give the council a chance to chime in," said Grace. "As to the meal plan, I'm not expected to serve nothing but burgers and dogs am I?"

Rebekah bumped her with her shoulder, "Wouldn't that make things easier?"

"I suppose, but..." Grace crinkled her nose at the thought. She wasn't exactly a gourmet chef, but she'd come a long way since that first Experience and liked to at least try to provide restaurant-quality food; better, even.

"The guests really liked making personal pizzas last Fourth of July," Rebekah reminded her, "you could always do that again. In addition to the barbecue you know we have to have."

Grace took a deep breath. "That sounds good. I'm sure the usual breakfast fare will work as well. Friday can be a leftover day, and then we can do pasta, subway-style sandwiches, and some kind of fish chowder or stew."

"Now seems like a good time to call the mayor and ask about setting up a meeting," said Molly. "I feel like we could all use a break."

Once again, she wanted to disagree but couldn't. If she were honest, wanting a family-only holiday wasn't just about the family-only part; she was tired. It had been a whirlwind of a year. She loved her new job and was incredibly grateful for the opportunity, but going from zero to sixty and then trying to maintain the sixty had taken a toll. Or maybe she was feeling sentimental about the approaching one-year anniversary of the first time she had opened her home as an inn. Looking back on the previous year, it was truly amazing how quickly things had changed in her life.

"Earth to Grace," Molly said, snapping her fingers to get Grace's attention. "Are you still with us?"

Grace shook her head to clear her mind. "Sorry, I was lost in thought. What were you saying?"

"Mayor Allen plans to call a meeting for this afternoon," she repeated. "Are you up for it?"

"Of course," Grace smiled. "Just tell me when, and I'll be there."

***

Three o'clock arrived much sooner than she'd expected. They'd spent the rest of the morning creating lists and making plans to shop and clean. After a quick lunch, it was time to go. Time always seemed to speed up when she was preparing for guests.

Everyone was already seated in their usual place when Grace and Rebekah arrived. Mayor Allan, Bea, Mr. Wilkins, Junior, and Addie sat in a circle, talking quietly as they waited.

"Oh good, you're here," said Mayor Allan as soon as they entered the room. "Are you ready to get started?"

Grace nodded her head in agreement. Mayor Allan was always quick and to the point. As the resident Mayor, Realtor, and Pastor, he was always in a hurry to move things along. "Thank you all for coming. We'll try not to take up more of your Sunday than necessary. I'm sure you've all seen the tree on my house," said Grace. When they all nodded, she continued. "We've been given an opportunity to host a family for Thanksgiving and are here to ask if any of you would like to be involved?"

"First of all," said Addie, "I'm really sorry about your house, and I hope you're able to get that taken care of quickly. Second, I am booked up for Thanksgiving, darlin', and cannot spare even a second."

That news was not unexpected. Addie's was the most popular diner in not just the town but the entire area. Not only did she serve food on the holiday, she sold pre-cooked heat-and-serve Thanksgiving meals throughout the week.

"I understand," she told Addie. "Anyone else?" she asked, her eyes scanning the room.

"You know we'd love to help," said Bea, referring to her and Junior. "But that storm hit us hard, too. Multiple fences are down, tree branches are everywhere, and it's just about all we can do to stay on top of it."

"Do you need us to round up a crew to help you guys out?" asked Grace. She was already scrolling through a list of people she could ask in her mind, and not for the first time did she sorely miss Jason and his football buddies.

Junior waved her off. "We can handle it," he replied, his tone gruff. "It's just gonna take a while, that's all."

Grace was sure that was his pride talking. After everything Junior had done for her, she was more than willing to repay the favor and might just have to force him to accept. But that was a problem for later. She turned to Mr. Wilkins, who was now her last hope. "Any chance you have some ideas?" she asked. She had to fight hard to keep the pleading tone out of her voice and was not altogether sure she was successful.

"I've got some games and puzzles I could sell you," he offered. "I also got a couple of novelty cheese making kits if that interests you?"

"That sounds great," Rebekah chimed in. "We will come by tomorrow to see what you have." She tugged on Grace's arm and leaned over to whisper in her ear. "This has been a colossal waste of time. We need to get out of here."

Unfortunately, Rebekah wasn't wrong, so a dejected Grace stood up, thanked everyone for their time, and headed out, Rebekah in tow.

"That was disappointing," she said once they were in the car and safely out of earshot. "I have never felt more let-down in my entire life."

Rebekah raised a brow. "That seems a bit dramatic. We knew going in this particular outcome was a possibility."

"I know, I was just hoping they would surprise me."

"Me, too, but it's okay; we can do this without them this time," replied Rebekah.

Grace started the car and turned in the direction of Cole's. "Can we, though? This will be our seventh holiday experience, and we've had their help and support for each one. Until now, that is. I don't think we have the time or the manpower to pull this off alone."

"There are other business owners in town, you know. There's no reason we can't branch out and look for help elsewhere."

Rebekah had a point. They'd already worked with some of the others in the past and could easily reach out again. In a town as small as Winterwood, business owners always looked for ways to bring in new customers. It was likely at least one of them would have some ideas and be willing to work with them.

"You're right," Grace replied, hope springing to life once more. "First thing tomorrow morning, we'll make the rounds and see what we drum up. In the meantime, we need to assemble a crew and help out Bea and Junior."

"I figured you would say that," said Rebekah, her phone in hand. "I've already sent out a text to everyone we know and arranged to meet at Juniors at four. That will only give us a couple of hours until dark, but if enough people show up, that should at least give us a good start. Right?"

Grace smiled at Rebekah. "Sometimes you truly amaze me, you know that?"

"That's a compliment, right?" she asked suspiciously.

"Yes, Rebekah, that is most definitely a compliment," Grace said sincerely. "And to answer your previous question, two hours should be enough time to at least get the fences repaired, which I'm sure is their number one concern."

Rebekah thought about that momentarily. "Shouldn't that have been the first thing they did? They could have cattle clear into the next county by now."

"Only if they had cattle in the field where the missing fences are," Grace explained. "I'm sure the first thing Junior did was move the cattle to a safe place. Besides that, he does more row cropping than cattle wrangling, so I'm sure that part at least wasn't as bad as you're imagining."

"That makes sense," she nodded. "Someday, I'll get used to all this farm business," she laughed.

"From what I've heard, someday is coming sooner than you think," Grace replied, nudging Rebekah with her elbow.

"Why do you say that?"

Grace rolled her eyes. "Duh! Didn't Thorne just buy that old farm on the other side of town? Before you know it, you'll be out there milking cows and churning your butter!" Grace teased.

"Is that what you plan to be doing at Cole's?" Rebekah shot back.

"You already know my job is to clean the horse poop," Grace said dryly. "Milking cows and churning butter would be a major upgrade."

They pulled into the driveway and parked in front of the house. "I'm going to check on Granny and then change into some work clothes," Grace told Rebekah. "Meet you back here in fifteen?"

"Sounds good to me," Rebekah replied. "Fingers crossed, this is a welcome surprise."

-Ten-

G race awoke to the scent of coffee and quickly hurried out of bed to catch Cole before he left for work. When she reached the kitchen, she saw him standing before the coffeemaker dressed in a warm flannel shirt, jeans, and work boots, his dark, curly hair still mussed from sleep. She walked up behind him and wrapped her arms around his waist, inhaling his scent as she laid her head against his back.

"Want to tell me why you're staring at the coffee pot like it holds the answers to all of life's questions," she asked softly.

He turned around and hugged her close, resting his head against hers. "I'm just tired," he replied.

"For some reason, I don't believe you." They stood there in silence, each lost in the quietude of the moment. "I'm sure going from living alone to a house full of people overnight has been difficult," she told him. "We can go to the hotel—

—Absolutely not," he interrupted. "That's part of the problem," he sighed.

Grace lifted her head to look at him. "I don't understand. What problem?"

Cole was not a man of many words but said what he meant and meant what he said. He was rational, level-headed, and chose to look for solutions instead of problems. So, if he felt there was a problem, there was major cause for concern.

"We're supposed to get married in little more than a month," he began, his hand moving in soothing circles on her back. "I had really hoped that you staying here while your house was repaired would unveil a clear path forward in regard to our living situation, but so far, all it's done is muddy the waters."

"I'm not sure I get what you mean?" she replied. "How has my staying here muddied the water?" Her arms tightened around his waist as she held onto him. She did not like where this conversation appeared to be headed.

He sighed, his head resting on top of hers again. "I just can't figure out how we're going to live together once we're married. You have so many people who depend on you on a daily basis that living here just does not make sense for you. And while I could, technically, live at the B&B with you, it isn't practical for me to be away from my farm. My fear is that even when we're married, we'll still end up living separate lives."

It wasn't easy, but Grace managed to push back the panic threatening to overtake her. "I can easily live here with you and go to the B&B each morning, just like I would if I had a job outside the home," she replied, a plan coming to mind. "There are a lot of people who can help ensure things run smoothly in my absence, including Rebekah, Molly, and Jilly. And if we have to hire an additional person, we can figure out a way to do that, too."

"At some point, Rebekah will move in with Thorne," he pointed out. "We can't depend on her forever."

"Rebekah and Thorne have only been dating for four months," she reminded him. "There are no guarantees they'll end up together for the long haul, and even if they do, I doubt wedding bells are in their future anytime soon." She leaned up to kiss him, her arms moving from his waist to his neck. "We can make this work," she whispered against his lips.

They took their time, neither wanting the rare moment of privacy to end. When they finally came up for air, Cole looked deep into her eyes.

"Thanks," he drawled, his left dimple showing as he smiled at her. "I feel like you brought me back from the edge."

"It's nothing you haven't done for me at least a million times," she replied dreamily, her gaze focused on his smile. "I kind of like being the voice of reason," she teased.

"It suits you," he teased back. He looked at his watch and grimaced. "Unfortunately, I need to go. I'm supposed to meet the contractor at your house later this morning. Any chance you can swing by to hear what he has to say?"

Grace nodded as she calculated how much time she would need to meet with the business owners downtown. Many businesses were closed on Mondays, so it was likely to take less time than she'd initially thought. "Call me when you're ready for me, and I'll be there," she told him.

"Will do." He poured the coffee into a thermos, kissed her cheek, then turned to leave. "I love you," he called over his shoulder.

"I love you, too," she called back. She watched him leave, then wandered over to the living room, where she found another fire waiting for her; Piper and Ruby curled up in their beds in front of it. A feeling of warmth washed over her as she surveyed the scene; Cole had done this for her. Why God chose to bless her with such a man, she didn't know, but she would spend every day for the rest of her life thanking Him for it.

It was too early to head into town, so she got to work on breakfast. Granny and Rebekah would be up soon, and the rest of the gang would likely be close behind. Despite everything, all was well in her world. She just hoped it stayed that way.

***

Grace and Rebekah parked at one end of the main drag. Their plan was to go door to door, up one side of the street and down the other, until they ended up back at their car. They got out and surveyed the businesses, each looking for the best place to start.

"We should probably skip the first one," said Rebekah. "It looks like it's still under construction."

"Good idea," Grace agreed. She looked at the second building and saw that it, too, appeared to be undergoing a remodel. "Huh," she said aloud. "That used to be an antique store," she said, pointing toward the former store. "I wonder what happened?"

Rebekah looked at Grace, her brow raised. "I wonder when all these changes started. It's only been a couple of weeks since Halloween, and I swear none of this construction was happening then."

"I have no idea," Grace shook her head in surprise. "How come no one's mentioned any of this? Have we all been so wrapped up in our own little worlds that no one has noticed all these changes?"

"I could see that happening with us," Rebekah mused, "but not Gladys. We may need to check on her. She's slipping in the gossip department!"

Grace laughed as she walked further down the street. They passed the aforementioned stores, a church, and a bank and then came to a stop in front of the building that used to house the local thrift store. "It looks like a new business is opening shop here, too. I wonder what it will be?"

Rebekah cupped her hands against the window and looked inside. "Looks like a coffee shop to me," she replied enthusiastically. "And whoever owns it appears to have money, as it looks like a place you'd frequent in Manhattan." She thought about that momentarily. "Specifically SoHo."

"That is oddly specific," Grace drawled. She stood next to Rebekah and peeked inside. "Hmm, I've never been to New York, but I believe you. This place is swanky!"

"Okay, Granny!" Rebekah teased. She stepped back and looked around for a sign. "I wonder when they plan to open? I will happily be the first customer."

Grace smacked her lightly on the arm. "Hey," she pouted, "what's wrong with my coffee?"

Rebekah resumed walking, Grace following close behind. "Nothing," she reassured Grace. "I'm just saying it would be nice to get a pumpkin spice latte once in a while. Or a mocha frappe," she took a deep breath and sighed, "You have no idea how much I long for my mocha frappes. It's the one part of my 'old life' I truly miss."

"You should have told me," Grace chided. "I could have tried to make them. If it's something you love, our guests might love them, too."

"That's true, but it's a big ask and something I can definitely live without," she put her arm around Grace's shoulders and gave her a sideways hug. "Trust me, you've done more than enough for me, and I couldn't be more grateful."

They reached the flower shop, Rustic Petals and Posies, and went inside to talk to Linda.

"Hey girls, what can I do for you?" Linda called out from the back of the store.

Grace and Rebekah weaved through the shelves full of rustic décor to get to the room where Linda created her floral arrangements. When they finally reached her, they found her knee-deep in flowers, cowboy boots, and vases.

Ribbons, glitter, and green mesh were strewn about as she made quick work of her latest creation.

"Isn't this adorable?" she asked excitedly, showing off the cowboy boot floral arrangement.

"Oh my gosh," Grace and Rebekah said in unison. They looked at each other and laughed.

"It is definitely adorable," Grace giggled. "What's it for?"

"It's a mock-up of a centerpiece for a wedding I'm doing next month," she replied.

Rebekah nodded. "Oh, this must be one of the options for Mike and Sally's wedding," she said, her interest in the centerpiece taking on new life. "Sally is going to love it!"

"I sure hope so," said Linda. "All she gave me to go on were the words 'rustic elegance'. While I obviously am all about 'rustic,' like all things, it's a matter of taste. Anyway, I assumed that's why you're here, but it looks like that's not the case. So, what can I do for you?"

"We're going to host a Thanksgiving Experience and are here to see if you might be interested in partnering with us this go around?" Grace explained.

Linda put the arrangement in her walk-in fridge and set to work on the next one. "That sounds intriguing; what did you have in mind?"

Grace gave Rebekah a helpless look. "Um, we were kind of hoping you might have some ideas."

"Well," she said, pausing to think, "I could always provide floral arrangements for your Thanksgiving table. Other than that, I'm not sure what more I have to offer."

Rebekah and Grace exchanged a look. "Do you know how many rooms Maisey booked?" Rebekah asked.

"I believe six," replied Grace.

Grace turned her attention back to Linda. "We'll take six flower arrangements for the rooms and 3 for the dinner tables. Is it possible to make them all like the one you did for Sally? These guests are looking for a traditional American experience, and I can't think of anything more American than cowboy boots."

"I thought we agreed football was the most American thing there is?" said Rebekah.

"We also said grilling hot dogs and hamburgers was the most American thing out there. So, I don't know, where does that leave us? Grilling burgers and dogs while wearing boots and playing football?" Grace said sarcastically.

Rebekah shrugged. "I'm from New York; how am I supposed to know?"

"New York is in America, too," Grace retorted.

"Yeah, but if you're going by that standard, the most American thing ever is a New York Yankee cap and a taxi. Neither of which I've seen down here," she said, her New York accent heavier than usual.

"Girls," Linda interrupted. "All of those things are 'American,' okay? There's no reason to argue. Now, I will gladly make your arrangements for you. When do you need them by?"

Thoroughly chastised, Grace and Rebekah dropped their argument.

"Saturday morning for the room ones, next Wednesday for the table ones," Grace mumbled.

"Sounds good," Linda nodded while making a note on her computer. "I'm sorry I couldn't be more help, but I'm sure you two will come up with something."

"Thanks, Linda," they replied in unison.

"You're welcome, see you Saturday."

They left the Rustic Posies and Petals and continued down the street, passing an old drug store, a construction business, and an office specializing in taxes before landing in front of a music store.

"Guitar lessons?" Grace asked hesitantly.

"It's an item on some bucket lists," Rebekah said skeptically, "but it might not be on their bucket lists. Let's put this one down as a maybe."

"Fair enough."

Next up was an old gift shop that had sat empty as long as Grace could remember, a telecommunications building, an old movie rental business, and then Cole's bar.

"Karaoke night?" Grace asked hopefully.

"Definitely," she grinned. "But we can talk to Cole about that later. Other side?"

"Other side," Grace repeated.

They crossed the street, passing by the hotel as they did so. Grace glanced toward it, saw that things looked as they should, then continued.

"What happened to Shelley?" asked Rebekah. "It's been a while since I've heard anything about her."

"After she went viral for her performance at the Haunted Hotel last Halloween, she decided to go to California to become a movie star," Grace explained.

Rebekah stopped to look at her. "Are you serious?"

"Unfortunately," she shrugged. "But who knows, maybe she really will become famous."

As they passed Bea's Bakery, Bea came out to greet them. "Thank you so much for helping us out yesterday," she gushed. "Junior is too stubborn to admit it, but it really was too much for us to handle alone."

"We were happy to do it," said Grace. She gave Bea a hug, then stepped back so Rebekah could do the same.

"I'm sorry I can't help with your new Experience," said Bea. "Even without the problems at the farm, I'm already inundated with orders for every kind of pie you can imagine."

She sounded exhausted, which worried Grace. Bea was younger than Granny and Gladys, but not by much. All of this back-breaking work had to be hard on her. "Is there anything we can do to help you?" asked Grace. "I already have to cook for the hotel; I can make extra pies if that will lessen some of your burdens."

Bea shook her head. "I can't ask you to do that, but I appreciate the offer."

"Okay, well, if you change your mind, the hotel has a nice new kitchen that has been fully inspected and is up to code," Grace offered.

They said their goodbyes, then went their separate ways. Next to Bea's Bakery was a real estate office, the VFW, then a barber shop.

"This is not going well," Grace said dejectedly. "We're almost to the end of the street, and all that's left are empty buildings, Mr. Wilkin's Five and Dime, and Chrissy's Boutique."

"There are a lot more empty buildings than I realized," Rebekah pointed out.

Grace grunted in reply.

"C'mon, Grace, cheer up; we only need four activities. Surely we can come up with four things to do."

"The kids will be off from school next week; what if we organized a community football game?" Grace asked hopefully.

Rebekah gave it some thought. "That could be fun. They could watch a professional football game one day and then play an amateur one the next. Do you know anyone you can ask to referee?"

"I'll call Conor and see if he can help me get in touch with one of the high school coaches. From what I've heard, the season is over for them, so they might be willing to help."

"That's a great idea!" she bumped Grace's shoulder with her own. "See, this isn't so hard once you put your mind to it."

"Easy for you to say," Grace mumbled.

They bought some puzzles and games from Mr. Wilkins and even a few cheese-making kits, just in case. Chrissy's was a bust, so they returned to the car.

"We still have four days to come up with three more ideas," Rebekah reminded her. "We'll go home, have lunch, and ask Google for help, okay?"

Grace texted Cole about the contractor, discovered the inspection had been pushed back to tomorrow, and decided to follow Rebekah's instructions. She almost turned down the street that led to her house, only remembering at the last second that she was staying at Cole's. This would take some getting used to.

Days till Thanksgiving

-Nine-

G race left early that morning under the guise of a before-school meeting with the high school football coach. In reality, she needed a break from the chaos. She loved her friends, but that many people in a small space was proving to be more than she could handle. Having grown up as an only child, Grace was used to peace, quiet, and lots of room to herself. Returning to Granny's spacious house would be a relief. On the other hand, leaving Cole's would be...well, she didn't want to think about it right now.

The first place she went was home to check on things. Thankfully, there hadn't been any additional rain since the storm, so she was hopeful that meant no further damage had occurred. She looked around inside and found nothing amiss until she inspected the ceiling in her bedroom and found water stains. This must have been what Cole had tried so hard to avoid telling her.

After she reassured herself the house was still standing, she went over to Addie's for a cup of coffee and a breakfast burrito. The place was full of the usual group of farmers drinking coffee and discussing the yield from this year's crops. According to them, it had been a really wet season, which meant...something. Based on their reactions, it was hard to tell if it was a good or bad thing. Some appeared to have lost crops to flooding, while others claimed to have the best yield of their lives. If she remembered, she'd ask Cole about it later.

Once she'd finished her breakfast, she left to go meet the coach. When she thought about it, it was a little crazy how few people she knew in a town as small as this; especially when you consider she grew up there. Gladys seemed to know everyone, but even she was slipping these days. When asked about the new businesses Grace and Rebekah had discovered in their walk around town yesterday, she'd been just as surprised as they'd been. The difference? Gladys would have answers by dinner time.

Grace parked in a visitor spot, checked in at the office, and was on her way to the gym. A trip that was more than a little nostalgic. Had it really been over eight years since she'd walked these halls as a student? Had she looked as young as the current students did? Somehow, she didn't think she did.

Coach Bryant was waiting in his office when she arrived. "Grace, I presume, glad to meet you," he said, shaking her hand with more force than necessary.

"Nice to meet you, too," she replied, resisting the urge to rub the soreness in her hand. "Did Conor fill you in on my proposal?"

"A proposal, eh?" he said, wiggling his eyebrows. "I'm afraid I'm already spoken for, young lady." He laughed heartily at his joke, stopping when he noticed Grace refused to join in.

How badly did she need his help? Was it worth putting up with this nonsense? She didn't think so, but they were running out of time and ideas.

"I was referring to the community football game over Thanksgiving break," Grace said sweetly. She pasted on her biggest smile and tried to remind herself that she'd be out of there and away from him before she knew it.

The coach was about to reply when someone knocked on the door. "Come in," he called out irritably. "Probably one of the students," he said to her. "I'll get rid of them."

That was not what Grace wanted to hear, and she sighed in relief when Conor poked his head in.

"Ah, there you are," he said to Grace. He entered the room and stood next to Coach Bryant, his taller form towering over the coach's shorter one.

Grace hid the smile that involuntarily took over her face when a look of discomfort appeared on the coach's. Both men appeared to be in their early thirties, but that is where the similarities began and ended. Conor, a former childhood actor, was tall, blond, and muscular, with an easy-going smile. The coach was short, bald, and currently had a disgruntled look on his face. While he did have some muscles, he looked like he spent his nights at the bar. Not that there was necessarily anything wrong with his appearance; she just couldn't help but see it through the lens of his bad behavior. But maybe she'd misjudged him. One lousy joke did not an evil man make.

"So, have you two already discussed the football game?" Conor asked them. He looked between the two of them, waiting for one of them to respond.

"I'd just asked about that when you arrived," Grace informed him.

They turned to look at Coach Bryant. "The school will never allow a non-sanctioned game to be played on school property," he told them. "Someone could easily get hurt in a game like that, and they will not assume that liability." The look on his face had turned to one of glee as he dashed their hopes.

"That makes sense," said Grace. "But what about at the park? We have community events there all the time."

His sour look quickly returned. "I guess that would work," he grumbled. "What exactly do you want from me?"

"I've already arranged with Principal Adams to borrow the portable bleachers, so what I need from you is help organizing the game, someone to referee, and someone to keep score. I can handle the rest," said Grace. She had already discussed her plan with some of the local food truck vendors who had agreed to cater the event.

"Fine," he relented. "I plan to be busy next week, but I'll talk to some other coaches and see if they are available. Will that make you happy?"

"Yes," Grace nodded. "Any chance we can do that now while I'm here? I really need to lock down these plans so I can finish making the arrangements."

He looked like he wanted to argue, but Conor put his arm around his shoulders and gave him a squeeze.

"You don't mind helping out my friend, right?"

Coach Bryant sighed loudly but gave in. "Give me a minute and I'll gather the troops." He shrugged off

Conor's arm and left the room, presumably to call for the other coaches.

"You're a lifesaver," Grace whispered to Conor when she was sure Coach Bryant was out of earshot. "That guy," she shook her head. "Is he always a jerk?"

"Pretty much. I should have warned you, but I was in the middle of something when you called. I had hoped to meet you as soon as you arrived this morning, but I got caught in the middle of a student argument and had to mediate. Sorry about that," he said sheepishly.

"You're here now," she said, letting him off the hook. "That's what matters. Is it bad I'm relieved he declined to participate?"

Conor shook his head. "I was counting on it."

They quit talking when Coach Bryant returned with several other men in tow. "This woman is looking for volunteers to work a community football game next week," he said, gesturing toward Grace. "Anyone interested? It's okay to say no. It won't be held against you."

Grace wanted to kick him in the shin for sabotaging her plans but was pleasantly surprised when the other guys gave an enthusiastic 'yes!'.

"Wow, thanks!" she said to the group. She pulled some pamphlets she'd created the night before out of her purse and handed them out. "Here's all the information you need to get started. If you have any questions, all you have to do is ask."

"I have a question," said Coach Bryant. When Grace raised a brow, he continued. "Are we done here? I have work to do."

It was still tempting to kick his shin, but she managed to refrain and instead walked out with the rest of the guys. "I really do appreciate this," she told them.

"If we took turns keeping score and refereeing, could we also play?" asked one of the men.

"I don't see why not," she replied. "This will be a community game, and all are welcome to play. I just need someone who knows what they're doing to help facilitate the parts I'm not good at."

One of the quieter ones spoke up. "We're going to need coaches," he told his colleagues. "I've got a couple of buddies who coach at the school in the town next door. If we get them involved, we should have enough people to rotate positions, so we'll all get a chance to play."

The others agreed with that plan, and since Grace didn't have any objections, she left them to their planning. "That went better than expected," Grace told Conor as they walked to her car.

"As long as we keep coach grumpy-kins at bay, I think this will be a hit," he replied.

"I really appreciate your help," said Grace once they'd reached her car. "How do you like it here? I feel like I haven't had a chance to talk to you since Easter!"

He cocked his head to the side. "Has it really been that long?" he asked. "I know we were both at the last two weddings, but I guess we haven't seen each other much since Easter. That's a shame, Grace. We should all hang out more."

"I agree," she said. "I'll call Cassie and Evie and try to arrange something soon."

"Sounds good," he looked at his watch and made a face. "I better get back to class. Good to see you again, Grace."

"You, too, Conor, thanks again!" she called out to his retreating back.

It was time to meet Cole and the contractor, so Grace headed back home. Hopefully, she'd get some good news. After her encounter with Coach Bryant, she could use some.

***

By the time Grace got home, which only took a couple of minutes, Cole and the contractor were already there. She hopped out of the car and rushed over, hopeful she hadn't missed anything important. When she reached Cole, he automatically put his arm around her waist and pulled her close.

"Hey, babe," he said, kissing the top of her head. "You remember Jim?"

Grace looked at the other man and took a moment to place where she'd seen him. "Oh, hey, you're the guy that fixed my roof last Easter."

He gave her a strange look. "It wasn't Easter, per se, but that was me."

"Sorry," she said sheepishly. "These days, I tend to view time relative to holidays. Occupational hazard," she laughed.

"No problem," he shrugged. "Cole and I were just discussing your roof access. It'd be easier for me if I could get up on the roof to see what I'm dealing with."

"I don't think we have access to the roof," replied Grace. She studied the man, who appeared to be in his mid to late thirties, with dark, shaggy hair, a matching beard, and the body of someone who'd spent his life doing physical labor. He was dressed like Cole but might be a little less patient if the look on his face was any indication.

"Have you ever been in your attic?" he asked.

"Yes," she replied. "I was up there last Christmas. That's where all the decorations are stored."

He rolled his eyes. "Did you happen to notice a ladder in the middle of the room?"

Grace really did not appreciate his tone. She usually had a lot more patience, but after dealing with Coach Bryant, she was down to nearly none. "No," she drawled, "I did not."

"Dude," Cole growled, "I know you're dealing with some stuff, but I'd appreciate it if you'd watch your tone with my fiancé."

The man stepped back and spent a moment breathing deeply. "I'm sorry," he said to Grace. "It's been a rough time, but that's no reason to take things out on you." He held out his hand. "I'm Jim," he said, shaking her hand.

"Nice to meet you, Jim; I'm Grace."

He nodded, a look of relief flooding his face. "Would it be okay if we took a look in the attic? I need to assess the damage there as well."

"Of course," she replied. She pulled her keys out of her purse and led them inside, up the stairs, and to the attic entrance that was located at the back of the house. "It's up there," she pointed at the trapdoor in the ceiling.

Jim pulled down the hidden staircase and climbed inside; Cole and Grace followed. A strangled cry escaped her lips when she saw the damage to not only the roof but all of the Christmas decorations she had stored inside. Branches were spread out throughout the space like tendrils clawing their way across the floor. Her beautiful nutcrackers were smashed to pieces, ornaments were strewn every which way, and lights lay shattered and scattered in every direction.

While Grace surveyed the damage, Jim worked his way to the middle of the room, stepping over her precious treasures like one would step through piles of garbage, which...she supposed, this stuff now was. She watched Jim pull down another hidden staircase.

"This is what I was looking for," he said to her.

She didn't trust herself to speak, so she nodded instead, then excused herself and hurried from the room. Once downstairs, she collapsed in a dining room chair and laid her forehead in her arms. Memories from last Christmas flooded her mind as tears flooded her cheeks.

When Cole sat next to her and pulled her into his arms, she went willingly, sobbing into his shoulder.

"It's all gone," she cried.

He rubbed her back in soothing circles, rocking her gently, much like one would a child. It was comforting, if not a bit embarrassing.

"It's okay," he whispered into her hair. "Things can be replaced. What's important is that you're okay."

"Those were Granny's childhood memories," she explained. "She's going to be devastated."

"I agree that she'll be sad," he said soothingly. "But you know what? This will give us an opportunity to make new memories."

Grace hiccupped, as she sat up to look at Cole. She took the tissue he offered and blew her nose. "What do you mean?"

"Well, how about you, Granny, and I go shopping for new decorations? We can even spend some time looking up vintage ones on the internet. How does that sound?"

"Amazing," Grace sobbed, a wave of fresh tears falling down her face.

Cole hugged her again and pressed a fresh batch of tissues into her hand. "If it's amazing, why are you crying, silly?"

"Because you're wonderful and I don't deserve you," she moaned against his chest.

Before Cole could reply, Jim appeared in the doorway. "Sorry to interrupt," he said, his voice gruff. "I've seen everything I need to see. If you give me a day or two to estimate materials, I'll get a quote for you as soon as possible."

"How long do you think it will take to do the repairs?" Grace asked. She kept her face hidden, not wanting the man to see her red, tear-stained skin and blotchy eyes.

"I don't know for sure, but it will be after Thanksgiving at the earliest."

Cole gently set Grace back on her chair, then stood to walk Jim out. When he returned, he pulled her back into his arms. "Now that that's done, what do you say we go home and spend some time looking at decorations with Granny?"

Grace nodded but held onto him when he stood and put her down on her feet. "I don't want to let go," she whispered.

"I have no intention of ever letting you go," he whispered back. "But Grace, please don't ever say you don't deserve me. It isn't true, and you know it."

"Fine, then I'm incredibly blessed to have you," she said instead.

Cole smiled at her, his dimples showing through his five o'clock shadow. "As I am to have you." He kissed her, then gently pried her fingers from around his neck. "Come on, baby girl, let's go home."

Grace took one last look around the house, then followed him outside. Home felt like a relative term these days, but as long as she was with Cole, that was all that mattered.

-Eight-

Grace awoke before the rest of the house, even Cole, which was almost unheard of. Careful not to wake Rebekah, she tiptoed out of the room, down the hall, and to the kitchen where she started the coffee pot. That done, she went to the living room and started a fire in the fireplace, smiling when she saw the animals curled up together on their beds and sleeping peacefully.

Once the fire was going, she grabbed a blanket and snuggled up in the middle of the couch so the pets, who were wide awake and happy to see her, could join her. Moments later, she had a dog on either side and Piper in her lap. As she sat absentmindedly stroking their fur, she tried to figure out what had her unsettled and unable to sleep. She'd had a wonderful time with Granny and Cole the day before, had managed to solidify the few plans they'd come up with for the guests, and had even gotten a head start on cleaning the hotel. So what was her problem?

As she sat there contemplating, Cole appeared, moved Max out of the way, and sat next to her.

"You're up early," he said, putting his arm around her and pulling her close. "Everything okay?"

"I think so," she said, unsure of how to respond. "Maybe I just needed some quiet time," she reasoned more to herself than to him.

"Should I leave you alone?"

Grace shook her head and snuggled closer to him. "Absolutely not, that's the last thing I want."

They sat there together in the silence. Just them, the dogs, and their cat. Their little family. These were the moments she cherished most.

"You never told me what was going on with Jim," she reminded Cole. "I'm assuming he isn't always a short-tempered jerk, or you wouldn't be friends with him."

Cole sighed and kissed her forehead. "This is just between us, okay? He doesn't need his business spread around town any more than it already is."

"You know I'd never gossip," Grace replied. "Accept for that one time, and it was for a good cause, I've never engaged in that behavior."

"I know; that's why I'm trusting you now," he said, kissing her again to smooth her ruffled feathers. "I just wanted you to know this isn't common knowledge, so you don't accidentally say something to the wrong person."

"Fair enough," Grace relented, letting him off the hook. She returned his kiss, then laid her head on his shoulder. "You may continue."

Cole chuckled, then let out a little sigh. "This is a long, messy story, so I'll try to keep it short and give you the highlights. Eight years ago, Jim met a woman, got her pregnant, and married her to give their son a stable, two-parent home. Unfortunately, their relationship has been nothing short of tumultuous."

"Basically, he married a Shelley?"

"In a sense," Cole agreed. "Bethany wasn't ready to become a wife and mother, so she's been in and out of their lives for the last seven years."

"Why does Jim keep taking her back?"

"For their son," Cole stated matter-of-factly. "Jim grew up in foster care and was determined to give his son the family he never had."

Grace's heart went out to Jim. If it hadn't been for Granny, that would have been her life, too. She owed so much to the woman who sacrificed everything to give her a loving home. "That's awful," she whispered as tears formed in the corner of her eyes. Every ounce of annoyance she'd felt for Jim evaporated.

"If you think that's awful, wait till you hear the next part," he growled.

She lifted her head to look at him, saw the anger flash in his eyes, and hugged him tight. "I'm almost afraid to ask."

He shook his head and took a breath to calm down. "Bethany came back to town a year ago and begged Jim to take her back. She promised she'd changed and wanted to be a real family again. Jim was hesitant but agreed. Cameron, his son, was in first grade and really wanted his mom in his life."

"I remember that age," said Grace, memories flashing before her eyes. "It was so hard to see all the other kids' moms in the classroom, helping out at parties and chaperoning field trips. Granny tried her best to make up for it, but it wasn't the same, and the other kids made sure I knew it."

"I'm sorry," he whispered against her hair. "But I'm sure that experience helps you empathize with Jim."

Grace nodded. "And Cameron," she agreed. "So, what happened?"

"For the six months or so, everything was great. But then Bethany hooked up with a high school coach and left them both again."

She gasped, her mind immediately conjuring up an image of Coach Bryant. Hadn't he claimed to be a 'taken' man or something else equally stupid just yesterday? He wasn't the only coach at the high school, but she could easily see him doing something gross, like hooking up with a married woman. She could not see why Bethany would choose a man like Coach Bryant over Jim. Having met both yesterday, Jim was the clear winner in her eyes, snappy attitude and all.

"I can see why this would be upsetting, but honestly, I think they're better off without her at this point."

"I'm sure Jim agrees, but that's not why he's upset. Apparently, the coach wants to be a daddy, so Bethany is suing Jim for full custody of Cameron."

Grace was so startled she jumped, the back of her head bumping into Cole's chin. "I'm so sorry," she said, kissing his chin. "Are you okay?"

Cole rubbed his chin with his hand. "I'm fine, how's your head?"

She felt the back of her head and winced. "I'll live," she replied. "I'm more worried about you."

"Honestly, I'm fine." He kissed her to prove he wasn't upset, then settled them down again.

In the chaos, Max and Ruby had retreated back to their beds and were now giving them puppy dog looks from across the room. Grace let out a small laugh, then sobered at the thought of what Jim was going through. "It seems unconscionable that a judge would agree to this after everything she's done," mused Grace. "Do you think she'll win?"

"Honestly? I don't know. Courts tend to favor the mother, but Jim has hired a good lawyer, so there's a good chance he'll at the least get shared custody. Sadly, good lawyers are expensive, and Jim isn't rich."

She'd been looking for a silver lining to her current house problems, and it appeared she'd found one. "Do you think the money from fixing my house will help him?"

"Every little bit helps," Cole replied. He looked at his watch. "I need to go, sweetheart."

"It's that time already?" she said sadly. They would have stayed on the couch together all day if it were up to her. But that wasn't practical, and she was nothing if not practical.

"I'll be home in time for dinner," he reassured her. "Maybe we could go out later, just the two of us?"

She smiled up at him, "I'd love that."

Cole leaned over and kissed her goodbye. "Then it's a date!"

Grace watched him go, then got up to start breakfast. She wished there was something she could do to help Jim, but outside of hiring him to fix her roof, there wasn't anything else she could think of to do. Hopefully, given enough time, she'd come up with something.

***

Rebekah and Grace sat in the living room, each on their laptops. "It's time to ask Google for help," Rebekah declared. She typed on her keyboard, then began to scroll. "Let's see what it says..."

"If you're seeing what I'm seeing, then all that came up was restaurants and Hobby Lobby," Grace replied. "Neither of which are helpful."

"Now, hold on a minute," she said. "I found a website with some ideas." She scanned the page, then faced Grace. "There's a drive-through light show, baking classes, ice skating, a holiday-themed crafting event—

—Let me see that," Grace turned Rebekah's laptop toward her and looked at the site. "All I see are Christmas activities," Grace complained. "We did everything on that list last Christmas. Ugh!"

Rebekah turned the screen back toward her and clicked a few buttons. "That's just one site. Give me a minute; I'm sure I'll find something."

Grace waited patiently but was sure this was a waste of time. Everyone she knew watched the big parade Thanksgiving morning, ate turkey, and then spent the rest of the day watching football. The days prior to the holiday were spent either shopping for the meal, preparing for the meal, or cooking the meal. What else was there to do? Nothing, that's what.

"Here's something," said Rebekah. "It says here 'Plays to see Thanksgiving week.'" She continued to read the page. "Never mind, the plays are Christmas-themed."

"Is it time to give up yet?" Grace asked.

Rebekah glanced at her over the screen. "That's not the attitude I have come to know and love from you," she teased. "Where's your fighting spirit?"

"It died," Grace deadpanned.

She rolled her eyes. "I thought I was supposed to be the dramatic one."

"You were, but then you became too pragmatic, so I had to pick up your slack," Grace replied.

"I'm choosing to take that as a compliment, anyway; what about these: Science City, Art Museum, or the Zoo?"

The options seemed worthy of consideration, but, if she were in another country, would she want to spend time at a museum or zoo? Maybe the zoo so she could see the native animals, but that was about it. "What kind of person comes here for Thanksgiving anyway?" she muttered. "Don't they have turkeys in Scotland?"

"It is odd," Rebekah agreed. "I could see coming here if they had family in the States, but visiting just because is weird."

"I'm about to take them bowling and call it a day," Grace joked. "Or, here's an idea: We're supposed to be known as the BBQ capital of the world or something; we can take them on a BBQ crawl."

"Is that supposed to be like a pub crawl, only with burnt ends and brisket instead of beer?"

Grace nodded emphatically. "Yes! What do you think?"

Rebekah tilted her head to the side as she considered it. "Sounds good to me," she nodded. "I still think the museums are a good choice as well."

"I agree. We can throw in a tour of the city and take them shopping at the Plaza."

"Hope they bring their wallets," Rebekah joked. "Thorne took me down there a few weeks ago, and it felt like I was back home in New York!"

Grace laughed as she entered their ideas on a spreadsheet. "I feel like this is enough for now. They may want to take a day to explore on their own or to rest before their flight home. I don't want to overwhelm them or us if I don't have to."

"So we're done for now?"

She closed her laptop and stretched. "We're done. Why? You have plans?"

"No, but I think it's time to tackle either the grocery or cleaning list. Time is flying by fast, and with only two of us, we can't afford to put this off for much longer."

Unfortunately, Rebekah was right. She'd already checked a couple of items off the cleaning to-do list, but there were many more to go, including laundering all the bedding, and that alone would take several days. "Let's work on the cleaning. We can do the shopping Friday."

Rebekah put her laptop in her computer bag and stood. "Sounds good. I'll grab my shoes and meet you at the car."

Grace checked on Granny, who was napping peacefully, with Piper curled up by her side, and Ruby at her feet. She looked around for Max, but when she didn't see him, figured Cole either came back for him or he left to find Cole.

She studied the room Granny was staying in and tried to imagine it decorated like her room at home. Could Granny be happy living here long-term? She'd spent her entire life at their home in town. Was it fair to even ask her? Grace hoped she had many more years with Granny, but time was fleeting and guaranteed to no man.

With a sigh, she turned to leave, careful not to disturb anyone on her way out. Heavy decisions would have to wait. Right now, she had a job to do; everything else would have to be put off until later.

Days till Thanksgiving

-Seven-

"Something sure smells good in here," Molly sang as she walked through the door of the hotel kitchen. "What are you making?"

Grace looked up from the pecan pie filling she was stirring on the stove. "I'm practicing pie recipes for Thanksgiving. I've also got some appetizers I've been working on," she said as she walked over to the fridge and pulled out a tray laden with crackers topped with brie, walnuts, and cranberry sauce. "What do you think?"

Molly took a cracker and popped it in her mouth. "Wow, these are delicious!" she exclaimed. "Seriously, Grace, your cooking skills have come a long way since last Christmas."

"Thank you," Grace blushed. For most of her life, the only thing she'd felt comfortable cooking was canned soups and sandwiches. Luckily, Granny was a fantastic cook and did all the cooking until she became ill and could no longer do it. Unluckily, it was at that time Grace had tried to take over and felt woefully unprepared. She wasn't sure what had changed in the last year but was grateful for whatever it was. "Where's Eliza," she asked.

"At the farm with Granny and Gladys," Molly replied. She popped another cracker in her mouth and moaned. "Don't worry, she's taking a nap," she explained when Grace gave her a questioning look. "She'd just gone down before I left, so I should have a couple of hours until she wakes up."

Grace nodded, her concentration on the task in front of her. She poured her filling into the pie crust, careful not to spill any. When she was done, she transitioned the pan to the oven, set a timer, and then turned back to Molly. "Do you have updates for me, or is this a social call?"

"Both," said Molly. She took a seat on a stool and then pulled out her phone. "I received an email from Maisey this morning with a couple of requests for the Thanksgiving meal."

"Oh boy," Grace groaned. "The only guest to ever make requests was Rebekah, and I'm not interested in going through that again."

"If I remember correctly, there were a couple of issues on Mother's Day, too," Molly reminded her.

Grace pulled out the ingredients for a pumpkin pie and set to work. "Pretty sure Rebekah was involved in that, too, and if she wasn't, she was there, so it still counts. Anyway, what does she want?"

Molly studied her briefly before turning her attention to the email. "She wants green bean casserole with the french onion things on top," Molly chuckled. "Her words, not mine. Cranberry sauce made with real cranberries, not the ones from a can, and the potatoes need to be smooth and creamy, not lumpy."

"Is that all?"

"Looks like it," said Molly, her eyes on her phone. She looked up at Grace. "That doesn't sound bad."

"I was planning to do that anyway, so we're good. Is that all you have for me?" Grace asked sharply. She winced a bit at her tone. She didn't mean to sound grumpy but found she was anyway. "Sorry," she apologized. "I guess I'm just a little stressed."

When Molly didn't respond right away, Grace glanced up at her and found she was staring. "What?" Grace asked. It was unnerving to be stared at, and she felt like she was on display.

"Is there anything I can do to help?" Molly finally asked. "I feel responsible for your stress and would like to do something to make it up to you."

Grace looked at her in surprise. "Why are you responsible? You didn't do anything wrong."

"Grant and I should have realized there was a problem with the insurance a long time ago," Molly sighed. "After all the hoops we had to jump through to get insurance on this place," she swept her arm to indicate the hotel, "at the very least, we should have verified the insurance on your house as well. It was negligent of us, and I'm sorry."

"I appreciate your apology, but it isn't necessary. We made a mistake, a very costly mistake, but it was just that, a mistake."

Molly sighed again. "Cole gave me the estimate from Jim. It's over fifteen thousand dollars and does not include repainting any of the upstairs ceilings."

The number should have been shocking. A year ago, it would have been shocking, but honestly, it was about what she'd expected. Tree removal was costly, as was a new roof. Add in structural damage, and she considered herself lucky she wasn't looking at twice that amount. The real question was: could they afford to pay it? "How much am I short?"

"Grant ran the numbers before I came over here, and if we include the payment for the Thanksgiving Experience, we should have enough to cover the repairs. However," she held up a hand when Grace began to express relief, "we will have no choice but to do another Christmas Experience to make up for the losses."

"Ah," Grace exclaimed, "now I understand. What you're really saying is that I need to postpone my wedding to Cole in order to keep the lights on."

She reached across the counter and put her hand on Grace's arm. "I'm so sorry," she said sadly, "I know how badly you want to get married I just don't know what else to do. We can't leave your house with a massive hole in it."

What was she supposed to say to that? Molly was right, and there was nothing else to it. That didn't make it any easier to swallow, however. All she wanted was to be alone, so she looked at her watch and then showed Molly the time.

"You better get back to the farm, Eliza should be waking up any minute now."

Molly looked like she wanted to argue, but stood instead. "Are you sure there's nothing I can do to help?"

"I need to do a taste-testing later today. If you and Grant want to come by the hotel for dinner, you can help me try out these recipes."

"That sounds good," Molly replied. She wiped at her eyes then grabbed her purse. "We'll be here around six. Will that work?"

Grace didn't trust herself to speak, so she nodded and busied herself with pouring the pumpkin mixture into the second pie crust. She allowed the tears to flow once she was sure Molly was gone. This was not at all what she'd expected to hear, but when she thought about it, it had been naive of her not to see this coming. But did she really have to give up her wedding? They didn't have to get married on Christmas Eve. As long as Granny and Cole were there, she'd be happy to get married on the front lawn of City Hall. In fact, she'd meet them there right now, flour-covered hair and all.

Later, she would talk to Cole and see what he had to say about it. For now, there was nothing but baking in her foreseeable future. The last thing she needed was unhappy guests, especially now when every penny counted.

***

It was almost time for the tasting party. Grace had just set the last tray on the buffet table when Cole came up behind her, circled her waist with his arms, and lifted her off the ground.

"Hey, beautiful," he said, kissing her on the cheek.

"Hey, yourself," she laughed. "What do you think?" she asked, sweeping her arm toward the table.

"It looks amazing," he replied, his eyes never leaving hers.

She laughed again, leaned back, and tilted her head for a proper kiss. When they separated, she turned to face him, her expression shifting from playful to serious. "I heard Jim sent you the quote," she stated.

Cole nodded. "I planned to talk to you about that after your party. How many people are coming?"

"It's just going to be the six of us," she explained. "Emilio and Vanessa are in Texas with his family, Evie and Jake already had plans with Conor and Cassie, and Jilly is out of town until the first of the month."

He pulled her close again, holding her against his chest as he massaged her neck and shoulders. "You seem stressed," he said quietly.

"Get a room, you two!" Rebekah teased as she and Thorne entered the room.

Grace and Cole pulled apart and turned to greet them. "Hey, guys," said Grace, her smile not quite reaching her eyes. "Help yourselves; all I ask is that you give me honest feedback when you're done."

She excused herself to check on things in the kitchen, even though everything was already set out on the table. What she really needed was a minute to herself to gather her thoughts. The moment she saw Cole, all the work she'd done to push down her feelings of sadness had quickly come undone, and now all she could think of was their canceled wedding.

Tears streamed down her face just as Rebekah pushed through the door.

"What's going on?" she asked. She grabbed a handful of napkins and handed them to Grace.

"I'm fine," Grace said, wiping her eyes. "Just a little overwhelmed."

"And I'm the Queen of France," she rolled her eyes. "Come on, Grace, I know you better than that. Whatever is going on, I'm sure we can come up with a solution."

Grace explained the situation as best she could, taking turns between talking and blowing her nose. "I don't know what to do," she said at last. "The rational part of me is trying to understand; my emotional part is so hurt and disappointed. I'm worried, Rebekah. I already didn't want to do this, and now that this has happened, I'm concerned I'm going to become so bitter and resentful that I'll treat our guests abominably and ruin everything."

Rebekah put her arm around Grace's shoulders and rested her head against hers. "First of all, I'm living proof that isn't possible," she said, squeezing Grace's shoulder. "There isn't a mean bone in your body, so don't worry about that. Second, there's no reason we can't get a little creative and have a wedding between the holidays. It won't be exactly what you had planned, but that doesn't mean it has to be any less special."

"What if Cole wants to postpone the wedding instead?" Grace whispered. If she were honest, that was her biggest fear. It was true they'd known each other for less than a year. And that it had also been less than a year since she'd thought a different man had been the other half of her happily ever after. But when she'd first met Cole, she'd known he was 'the one.' And yes, there were those who thought that was naive and silly, but he'd spent every day since reinforcing her beliefs through his actions. She was utterly and madly in love with him.

"I've seen the way he looks at you," said Rebekah. "I would bet my last dollar he won't."

"Thanks," Grace sniffed and wiped her nose again. "I guess we need to get back out there and see what everyone thinks of the food."

"I hope I'm not too late to try those cracker things you made," Rebekah joked. "They look delicious, and I won't be surprised if I have to fight for the last one!"

Grace surprised them by reaching over and hugging Rebekah. "You're a really good friend," she whispered. "I don't know what I'd do without you."

Rebekah hugged her back. "I feel the same." She stepped back, an awkward look on her face. "I'm not good at this," she said sadly. "But I really appreciate everything you've done for me. I have a chance at a real life because of you. This wedding is a way for me to repay you, so I promise I will do everything I can to make it the best day of your life."

For the second time that day, or was this now the third? Tears streamed down Grace's face. "You're making me cry again," she laughed.

"Yeah, well, now I'm crying, too," she replied, joining in on the laughter. "We're quite the pair," she said, grabbing another handful of napkins and passing half to Grace.

They dried their tears and did their best to repair their make-up or, at the very least, not look like they'd just been to a crying fest.

"We really need to get back out there," said Rebekah. "I wasn't kidding about those crackers, and after the way Molly looked at them before I left, I'm pretty sure I'm already too late.

Grace walked over to the fridge and grabbed another tray off a shelf. "Here you go," she said, handing it to Rebekah. "Your own personal snack plate."

Rebekah's eyes went wide. "Wow, thanks!" She popped one of the crackers in her mouth and moaned. "They're even better than they looked out there. What's the secret?"

"I added some spices to the cranberry sauce," Grace explained. "And candied the walnuts. I thought it would enhance the flavor and pair well with the cheese."

"Well, you thought right! Once our esteemed guests get a taste of these, they'll forgive a multitude of sins," she joked. She ate several more, then put the tray back in the fridge. "I'm not sharing," she said to Grace's raised brow. "When it's time to leave, I'm going to grab them and sneak them back home!"

"Looks like there's at least one 'yes' vote on the appetizer," nodded Grace. "That is good to know."

"Now we really need to get back out there. For all we know, a fight has broken out over these, and we need to break it up!"

Grace linked arms with Rebekah and followed her to the dining room. It was hard to imagine less than a year had passed since they'd first met. And even harder to imagine their relationship had started out on such bad terms. She honestly couldn't imagine her life without Rebekah and hoped she never had to try.

-Six-

Grace walked into the living room and looked around. "Oh good, you're all here," she said once she saw Molly, Grant, and Gladys had arrived. "I just received an email from Carl informing me that he and his sister, Katherine, would like to spend Christmas with us again."

"What about his brother?" asked Granny. "Is still unwell enough to travel?"

"Sadly, he passed away a few weeks ago," Grace replied. "But Carl assured me Edward went peacefully and that while they are sad, they are grateful for the time they had together."

Gladys, who was sitting next to Grace on the couch, reached over and squeezed her hand. "I'm proud of you," she beamed. "Me and Josie both."

Granny nodded her agreement. "It was a risk reaching out to Carl's estranged siblings, but it paid off. Without you, he would have lost the chance to reunite with his brother before he passed. You gave them the gift of time, my darling girl. Me as well."

Grace's cheeks reddened at the unexpected attention. "I just did what anyone would do," she demurred.

"That's not true," said Grant. "We all had the opportunity to do what you did, yet none of us even considered it." He got up, kissed Molly and Eliza, then walked over to Grace and hugged her. "Take the win," he teased, "you earned it."

Grant waved goodbye to the room, then left for work just as Cole was coming in. When Grant saw Cole, he walked back inside with him. "I need to hear this story," he joked. "Work can wait."

Cole frowned, then looked down at his mud-covered clothing. "Cow fell in the mud," he deadpanned.

"Did it take you with it?" asked Rebekah. "Cause right now, you're more mud than man."

He shook his head, irritation on his face clear to see, even through the mud. "The storm created a mud-hole in one of my pastures, and when I moved the herd over, one of the cows fell in and got stuck. Riley and I just got it out." He looked around awkwardly for a moment before excusing himself to get cleaned up.

"That was interesting," mused Molly. "Does this kind of thing happen often?" she asked Grace.

"Not that I've seen," she replied. "But I'm not exactly an expert on these things." Grace excused herself and went to the kitchen to make Cole some hot coffee and a breakfast burrito to-go. She knew he would need both when he was finished cleaning up. The food was just about done when he appeared in the doorway.

"You're a lifesaver," he replied gratefully. He took a drink from the thermos and then grabbed the burrito. "What are you up to today?"

"Rebekah and I are going shopping, and then it's back to the hotel for last-minute cleaning and meal prep. Why? Do you need me for anything?"

Cole smiled and pulled her close. "I always need you," he whispered against her hair. "I was just wondering if you might have some time to spend together tonight, seeing as how it's the last night before the guests arrive."

"I'll make time," she said quickly.

He chuckled, then gave her one last hug. "Meet you here around six?"

Grace nodded. "I'll be ready when you are." She needed to talk to him about something, but she couldn't remember what it was. After a moment of thought, it popped into her head. "By the way, we never talked about Jim's estimate. Did you give him the okay to start work?"

"Not yet. I wanted to talk to you about it first, but I forgot all about it. Did Molly give you the details?"

"If by details you mean the price, then yes," Grace informed him. "I don't think we have a choice, so please tell him to start as soon as possible." She wanted to talk to him about the wedding but knew this wasn't the time. Perhaps tonight they could have that particularly painful conversation, or maybe another time when they weren't so busy and stressed out.

"Are you sure?" he asked hesitantly. "Several of the upstairs rooms were damaged by water, and the ceilings need to be repainted, which is not part of the estimate. We can always get another quote from someone who is willing to do all of the work."

Grace considered that, but then remembered the difficult time Jim was going through. "No, I want him to do the work. I can paint the ceilings myself," she said with a confidence she didn't expect. The Grace from a year ago would never have said that. That Grace didn't believe she was capable of anything but failure. This Grace, on the other hand, had spent the summer painting most of the hotel and knew she was capable of doing the job. What a difference a year could make.

"If you're sure," he replied. He pulled his phone out of his back pocket and scrolled through his contacts. When she nodded, he pushed the call button and headed out. "I'll let him know," he called over his shoulder. He waved on his way out, then he was gone.

From the looks of things, Grant was also gone, so Grace felt it was time to head out as well. "Are you ready to go?" she asked Rebekah.

"Ready as I'll ever be," she said.

"Anybody need anything while we're out?" Grace asked. She grabbed her purse and keys, and when everyone said, "no", she walked out the door, Rebekah close behind.

They were on the road and on their way out of town when Rebekah spoke up. "Any chance we can grab one of those coke and hot dog specials for lunch?" she asked hopefully.

"That's the best part of the trip," Grace joked. "It would feel like a crime if we didn't!"

"Would that make us Thelma and Louise?" she asked, a wry smile on her face.

Grace laughed. "If we're going that route, I hope it's over something much more exciting than a hot dog and a coke!"

"Time will tell," Rebekah replied cryptically.

***

Grace was ready to go at six o'clock sharp. She was ready much earlier than that, but she tried to act natural so Cole wouldn't realize she'd been chomping at the bit all day to get some alone time with him. By the time he was ready, she'd fed Gladys and Granny, let the dogs out to run around and do their business, and said goodbye to Rebekah, who was out on her date with Thorne. When they left, Granny and Gladys were happily watching their favorite game show while eating dessert, and Grace couldn't help but wonder if that would one day be her future as well.

"Finally," she said, scooting over to the middle of the truck seat to sit next to him. She laid her head on his shoulder and closed her eyes while he drove them to the hotel. He had planned to take her to a restaurant in the city, but she hadn't wanted to waste time on the drive and instead suggested a romantic dinner for two in the hotel kitchen. Not to mention, if she were honest, this was one last opportunity to test out a couple of recipes before the guests arrived tomorrow; not that he needed to know that.

When they arrived, she hopped out of his side of the truck and led the way inside, stopping long enough for him to admire all the cleaning they'd done earlier in the day.

"It looks great!" he said enthusiastically. "Are you ready for tomorrow?"

"Yes," she nodded, resuming the walk to the kitchen. "Everything is ready except for the flowers, but Linda is supposed to deliver those before the guests arrive."

He paused outside the kitchen door and took her hands in his. "How do you really feel about doing this last-minute Experience?" He watched her face while rubbing circles on her palms with his thumbs.

Grace found it difficult to concentrate when he did things like that, but she did her best to answer him honestly. "I was hoping for a break, but I'm trying to have a positive attitude and make the best of it." She tried to smile but failed miserably when the image of their wedding popped into her head.

"What's wrong, darlin'?" he asked. He let go of her hands to wrap his arms around her waist. "It can't be that bad, can it?"

"We have to cancel the wedding," she blurted out. Tears threatened the corner of her eyes, but she held them back, not wanting to appear weak or childish in front of Cole. An emotion that looked like pain mixed with surprise crossed his face, and she immediately wished she could take back her words.

"Why?" he whispered.

In Grace's mind, Cole was the equivalent of Superman. Strong, steady, hard-working, kind, honest, and incredibly sexy. So, it was still somewhat shocking to her to see he was also vulnerable and just as capable of being hurt as she was, and right now, this crazy man actually appeared to believe this was something she wanted as if that could ever be possible.

"When Grant ran the numbers on the house repairs, he discovered that while we can afford it, we'll need to do a Christmas Experience to make up for the financial hit we're going to take. Which means our wedding cannot move forward as planned."

"Is that the only reason?" he asked, his face now showing very little emotion.

"Are you serious?" she exclaimed loudly, startling them both. "Of course it's the only reason. I'm over here devastated by this turn of events and—

Cole silenced her by closing the distance between them and kissing her. When he finished, he held her close against his chest; his arms encircled tightly around her waist.

She wasn't sure how long they stayed that way, but it wasn't nearly long enough, and she strongly objected when he let go.

"Let's talk this over while we eat," he suggested. "I'm starving," he chuckled.

"Any more cow incidents?" she asked, reminding him of his earlier mishap.

He winced and shook his head. "No, thankfully, and I hope it stays that way. But they're predicting another storm tomorrow night, so I ain't holding my breath."

When Grace was there earlier, she'd arranged a candlelight dinner at a little table in the corner of the kitchen. She gestured for Cole to take a seat while she lit the candles and poured them each a glass of wine she'd had chilling on ice for the occasion. "I don't remember this being a problem before," she mused. "Or have I just been out of the loop?"

Cole took a sip of wine and shook his head. "This year has been a lot wetter than last year," he explained, "but Grace, I find it hard to believe you're that interested in this. Can we please talk about the wedding instead?"

She busied herself by heating up their dinner, which consisted of Shepherd's Pie Soup, a hearty Italian Bread Loaf, and a spinach salad with candied walnuts, fresh strawberries, and blueberries. If he liked the meal, her plan was to serve it to the guests on their first night there.

"Earth to Grace," Cole said, waving his hand in her direction.

"Sorry," she mumbled, placing the dishes on the table. She sat down and faced him once everything was arranged to her liking. "I don't know what to do," she admitted. "I try so hard to solve everyone else's problems, but I have no idea how to solve my own."

He reached across the table and clasped her hand in his. "What would you like to do?" he asked gently.

"If it were up to me, I would marry you right now," she replied. "But it's not just me. There's you, Granny, and even Rebekah to think of. Not to mention all of our friends who've been so supportive." She sighed and looked down at the entwined hands. "I don't want to let anyone down, but I don't want to wait forever to become your wife, either."

"I'll happily call Allan and get him down here right now if that's what you really want?" he replied. "Everyone who loves you would understand."

"Even Granny?" asked Grace. "She's been looking forward to this day since I was a little girl. It's her dream to make my wedding dress, and she's already halfway done. I can't deprive her of that."

Cole nodded, understanding clear on his face. "In that case, we'll just have to move the wedding up. How about two weeks from tomorrow?"

Grace's head shot up, her mouth open in surprise. "Are you sure? You've always told me I shouldn't rush things. I was convinced you'd see this as a reason to postpone the wedding indefinitely."

"I think we've waited long enough," he drawled. "You'll be busy all next week, though. Are two weeks asking too much? Should we make it three?"

"I'll talk to Granny and Rebekah and see what they say," Grace said excitedly. "If they think we can be ready in two, then I'm going to hold you to it!"

His adorable dimples appeared, his eyes twinkling in the candlelight. "Wild horses couldn't keep me away," he laughed. "My stomach, on the other hand," he laughed again before digging into the soup with gusto.

Grace watched him eat, interested to see how he reacted. Cole was not a hard man to please and would eat just about anything she put in front of him to avoid hurting her feelings. Luckily, she knew him well enough to read to the subtle cues he gave when he was just being 'nice.'

"This is the best soup I've ever had," he said between mouthfuls. "And this bread," he tore off a piece and dipped it in the soup, "they pair so well together." Within minutes, his dishes were clean. "Any chance there's enough for seconds?

She could not have asked for a better reaction. The soup was definitely a winner. "Of course," she said, getting up to get him another bowl.

After dinner, they strolled arm-in-arm down the main street, past his bar and the rest of the businesses. It was late enough that everyone had gone home for the day, the empty street peaceful and quiet. And now that the business of their wedding had been settled, she felt relaxed enough to enjoy it.

When they arrived back at the hotel, Grace made sure everything was locked up, then hopped in the truck next to Cole.

"Ready to go home," he asked.

She smiled up at him. "Ready."

Days till Thanksgiving

-Five-

G race arrived at the hotel an hour before the guests were expected. Rebekah was busy at a wedding, so Grace was flying solo, her nerves slightly on edge. Then again, she always felt this way right before meeting her guests for the first time. Welcoming strangers into her home was a strange experience. The fact that she was at the hotel and not the B&B made little difference. For the next six days, she was responsible for ensuring people she'd never met had the best experience of their lives. Which, in her opinion, was no small feat. Okay, that might be an exaggeration, but she still felt pressured to keep her guests happy.

When Linda arrived with the flower arrangements, Grace met her at the door, excited to see that the cowboy boots looked even more adorable than she'd remembered. They looked rustic and charming on the nightstand next to the bed, a perfect accent to the décor she had worked so hard on modernizing over the last few months. It was hard to believe how far this place had come from the sixties relic it had started as when they first bought the hotel.

"You should come down to the store sometime," Linda said on her way out. "I have some things I think will help pull together what you've done here," she offered. "It's the little things that make all the difference."

"I would love that," Grace said, inwardly groaning. She would love to take Linda up on her offer, but at this point, she could only see dollar signs floating out the window. "I may have to wait until after the holidays, but I will definitely be by as soon as possible."

Linda nodded and smiled. "No worries, darlin'; you know where to find me!"

Grace said her goodbyes and let out a sigh of relief. She checked her watch, thirty minutes to go and counting. She got to work arranging trays of appetizers on the buffet table in the lobby, along with tea, coffee, and bottles of water. That done, she walked through the rooms one last time, looking for any signs of dust and making sure each room had plenty of extra blankets and fresh towels. She'd wanted to make those cute little animals out of the hand towels but had given up in frustration. That appeared to be one skill she was not going to master.

The arrival time came and went, though Grace was not surprised. Winterwood was off the beaten path, and it wasn't exactly uncommon for out-of-towners to miss their exit and have to double back. Plus, she reasoned, her guests could have stopped for something to eat, their plane could have been delayed, or any number of things could have caused the delay.

A full hour passed, and Grace began to question her decision to put out the appetizers. She was about to put them back in the fridge when she heard a car outside. Several minutes later, the door opened to admit a man, woman, and two young children. They looked so frazzled that Grace rushed to meet them, quickly offering to assist with their bags and directing them toward the snacks.

"Oh, thank you," the woman said as she helped the kids with a bottle of water and an assortment of snacks. "This has been the longest trip of our lives," she laughed. "We were going to stop for food but couldn't find anywhere to eat!"

"Not to mention how difficult it was to get used to driving on the wrong side of the road!" the man exclaimed. "Luckily, I caught on after a wee bit of honking from the other drivers."

Grace was horrified at the thought her guests could have been injured on the way here. "I'm so sorry," she said, her hand on her heart. "I should have offered to pick you up from the airport. It never crossed my mind how different things would be for you here."

"Ach, nay," he said with a wave of his hand. "It's good for us to have the experience. Something to brag about to the fellas back home."

Their Scottish accent was light but charming. Grace felt she could listen to them talk all day, but, thankfully, she was raised to have better manners than that.

"Let me get you checked in," she offered, "I'm sure you'd like to get settled in before dinner."

"Aye, that would be lovely," said the woman. "I'm Brianna; this is me husband, Maxwell," she said, pointing to the man, "and our boys Aidan and Caden," she pointed to the two adorable red-headed boys.

"Aww, we have a dog named Max," Grace exclaimed, quickly slapping her hand over her mouth when she realized what she said. "I am so sorry, I didn't mean it like that."

Maxwell guffawed at her gaffe. "Don't worry, lassie; I'm sure he's just as studly as I am, too!"

Brianna slapped her husband's arm and rolled her eyes. "Stop giving Grace a hard time," she teased. "Ignore me, husband," she told Grace. "He thinks he's the next Craig Ferguson. Ye know who that is, right?"

Grace nodded, a bemused smile crossing her lips. "I do," she laughed. She grabbed their key and motioned to them. "Right this way."

Once they were settled, Grace returned to the lobby and waited for the next guests to arrive. An older man and a teenage boy came next. The elder was a tall man with a shock of white hair she suspected was once red. He had an easy smile and was somewhat loud and boisterous.

"Evening, lassie!" he said, plopping down on one of the chairs. "Me names, Hugh, and this here mopey lad is me son, Logan," he pointed to the surly-looking teenager beside him.

"Nice to meet you both," she said, coming round the desk to shake their hands. "Please help yourself to some refreshments. Your rooms are ready as soon as you are."

Hugh got up to retrieve a plate of food and some coffee, then returned to his seat. "We've got one more car-full to go before we're all accounted for," he told her.

"Not a problem," Grace told him. She wanted to ask more questions but didn't want to appear rude since he'd just arrived. So, she excused herself and returned to the desk.

When the door chimed a third time, she looked up to see a beautiful young woman with long, dark brown hair and large brown eyes enter the lobby. And right behind her was none other than Hunter and Amelia Parish.

Grace dropped the bottle of water she was holding; the loud thud when it landed on the granite floor caused everyone to look in her direction. Anger clouded her judgment, and she was just about to let Hunter have a piece of her mind when he and Amelia rushed to the desk to confront her.

"Please," begged Amelia. "Give us time to explain before you say anything."

"I'm listening," said Grace through gritted teeth.

Amelia gave her a horrified look. "Not now," she whispered. "Later, when no one else is around."

The last thing Grace wanted to do was become complicit in yet another one of Hunter's duplicitous schemes. But she had bills to pay, and honestly, once her initial anger faded, she decided she didn't care. "Fine," she said sweetly. She picked up the room keys and handed them to Amelia and Hunter. "Rooms are down the hall and to your left."

Maisey chose that moment to come up behind them and wrap an arm around each of their shoulders. "Isn't this great!" she said excitedly. "It's exactly as I imagined it to be, only better! Rebekah's pictures don't do this place justice. Not that she's not a brilliant photographer," she added quickly. "Just that it's hard to capture the essence of a place in a photo, ye know?"

Grace nodded, somewhat amused by the woman's exuberance for their humble hotel. She handed her a room key. "If you all will follow me, I'll show you to your rooms.

She led the way down the hall, pausing briefly to show them the bathrooms. When she got to their rooms, she directed them to the correct one and then tried to excuse herself. "Dinner's at six," she informed them. "The dining room is through the lobby, but I'll meet you there to show you the way."

"Will Rebekah be there?" asked Maisey. "I'm dying to meet her."

"Sadly, Rebekah is working elsewhere today, but she should be around tomorrow," replied Grace. "And I'm sure she'll be just as excited to meet you." Grace stared pointedly at Hunter as she said the last part.

"Wait?" he said before she could leave. "Rebekah's here? In Winterwood?"

Grace gave him a quizzical look. Judging by the way his girlfriend spoke of Rebekah, her presence in Winterwood should not have come as a surprise to him.

"Yes," Grace stated. She purposefully chose not to offer any additional details, just to make him squirm uncomfortably.

"But why?" he asked nervously. "I thought she lived in New York?"

Maisey turned to Hunter. "I told ye she lived here, silly," she rolled her eyes and turned to Grace. "I don't know why he keeps insisting she would never live somewhere like here. I've been telling him for months that she's made Winterwood her home."

"How long have you been following Rebekah on social media?" Grace asked, genuinely curious.

"Oh, I don't know, at least a few years," she shrugged. "I loved following her travel blog, but things got really interesting when she settled here. She became more, how do you say? Real? When Hunter told me about his family holidays, I knew we had to come here to celebrate with him. And this was the perfect place to do it!" she flung her arms out and twirled excitedly.

"You can be sure I will let Rebekah know her biggest fan is staying here at the hotel," Grace drawled.

"Thank ye," Maisey sang out as she entered her room.

Grace smirked at Hunter, then turned on her heel and left. If he wasn't squirming before, he was sure to be now. The only thing worse than running into one of your exes was to run into two of them. And she would know. She once had to host two of her biggest enemies in her own home. They might not have been her exes, but the concept was the same.

She'd just returned to the lobby when Hunter appeared hot on her heels.

"You can't be serious," he screeched. "What is Rebekah doing here? She's supposed to be in New York. You know, as far away from here as she can get."

"Well, Hunter," Grace snapped. "She's here because after you abandoned her, her parents disowned her and left her with no money, nowhere to live, and no way to take care of herself. So she moved in with me."

"She lives with you," he sputtered. "Rebekah Rutherford, the New York socialite, lives here, in this podunk town; with you?"

"I don't think I appreciate your tone," Grace drawled.

He ran his hand through his hair and began to pace. "This isn't happening," he moaned. He stopped and grabbed Grace's hands. "You have to help me," he said, pausing when he felt the ring on her hand. A look of shock came over his face when he turned her hand over and saw the diamond. "You're engaged," he accused.

This whole scene with Hunter would have been comical if it weren't so insulting.

"Yes," she stated flatly.

"To whom?" he snarked. "The cowboy? Or did you find yet another man to dally with after I left?"

"That's a bit rich coming from you," Grace replied. "From what I've seen, you haven't changed one bit. Still lying, still playing games. You're too old for this, Hunter."

Hunter sneered at the mention of his age. "You didn't answer the question."

Grace rolled her eyes. "I'm not dignifying that with a response."

"Whatever," he muttered. He turned on his heel and stomped away. "You better not say anything to Maisey," he called over his shoulder.

"Or what?" she asked.

"Or you'll regret it," he spat.

She watched him go, shaking her head as he went. A part of her had known this was coming, but boy, if she didn't wish it'd been wrong. This was going to be a long week. At least she had her wedding to look forward to. That was something not even Hunter could take from her.

-Four-

"**A**re you awake?" Grace whispered from her side of the bed. It was dark out, the light from the moon barely bright enough to illuminate Rebekah's outline next to her.

"Yes, why?" Rebekah said sleepily. "Is something wrong?"

Grace knew she should wait until morning to drop the Hunter bomb on Rebekah, but her nerves wouldn't let her rest until she'd warned her friend he was back in town. "Hunter's here," she said nervously.

Rebekah bolted up in bed and flung her covers on top of Grace. "What? Where?"

"Not here, as in, in this room, here in Winterwood," Grace explained. "He showed up at the hotel with Maisey and her family. Amelia, too."

She pulled the covers back over herself and laid back down. "You shouldn't scare people like that," she said. "You could have given me a heart attack."

"That's how I felt when he walked into the lobby, although I suppose I did expect it to happen."

"I don't blame you," she said. "I guess we both get to tell a big, fat 'I told you so' to Molly," she joked. "How did it go when you met Maisey? Was she hostile toward you?"

Grace was surprised Rebekah assumed Hunter had been honest with his newest girlfriend, given how he'd treated them. "She doesn't know," Grace explained. "Amelia and Hunter ambushed me when they got there and begged me not to say anything. It was...strange."

"I can't believe Amelia would go along with that," said Rebekah. "Nor do I understand why they're even here."

"Maisey mentioned something about Hunter's family holidays, and I've been wondering if he told her lies similar to the ones he told me," Grace replied. "She may be trying to recreate those for him, though she did seem to be just as interested in you as she is in him. She's your biggest fan," Grace teased. "Hunter, on the other hand, is terrified of you. He almost had a heart attack when he found out you lived here."

"That's because he knows I would have ripped him a new one had I been there," she said dryly. "There's no way I'm going along with his little charade. People have pasts; there's no reason he can't be honest with Maisey and tell her I'm his ex-fiance."

"There's no reason he couldn't have told her that when she first mentioned you," Grace corrected. "Now that all this time has passed, it's going to be pretty hard to explain why he lied about it."

Rebekah laughed bitterly. "He hasn't changed a bit, has he?" She laughed again, this time her laugh a little more joyous. "Imagine taking your new girlfriend to spend the holiday at an inn owned by one ex-girlfriend, only to discover that your ex-fiance works there too. And you never bothered to inform the new girlfriend about either of them. What was he thinking? Does he really think he can keep this from her? Or that we'll go along with it?"

It was Grace's turn to laugh. "I think that's exactly what he thinks."

"Does Cole know?"

"Not yet," Grace sighed. "He came home late, and since we didn't have much time together, I didn't want to waste it talking about Hunter. I hope he doesn't get upset and think I purposely hid it from him when he finds out."

"If I were you, I'd tell him first thing this morning. You don't want him to have any doubts about your feelings," she said.

Rebekah was right; that was the last thing Grace wanted. She tried to remember how she felt the second she saw Hunter come through the door. Had there been even a hint of feelings for him? All she remembered was rage, and even that had burned out quick. So yeah, she was definitely over him, likely had been since the first moment she'd met Cole.

"What does she look like?" Rebekah asked curiously.

"The exact opposite of us," Grace said with a laugh. "I thought men were supposed to have a 'type'? Judging by how different Valerie and I are, maybe that's not true."

"Maybe they look for women with similar characteristics over similar looks, but that wouldn't be true for those two either," Rebekah joked. "Valerie and I have far more in common than you and she ever will."

Grace pshawed. "A love for expensive shoes does not make you two peas in a pod," she drawled. "Besides, that was old Rebekah; new Rebekah prefers to rock cowboy boots, remember!"

"New Rebekah can still appreciate a good Louis Vuitton when she sees one," she retorted. "She just can't afford them," she joked. "Anyway, we should try to get some sleep before the fireworks are set off later today."

"I'm assuming you mean metaphorically, and there isn't really a fireworks show planned for later tonight?"

Rebekah rolled over and pulled the covers over her head. "Sorry to disappoint girlfriend, but I still promise to put on a good show.

Grace had zero sympathy for Hunter but she did feel bad for Maisey. She'd had been heartbroken when she'd found out Hunter had lied to her last Valentine's Day; she couldn't imagine how Maisey would feel, especially after flying halfway around the world for him. Then again, maybe she would forgive him. He wasn't cheating on her; he'd just lied about his ex-girlfriends.

She tried to imagine how she would feel if she were in Maisey's place and found out Cole was keeping secrets from her. On the surface, it seemed innocent enough, but then you had to wonder why he lied. Grace believed she would forgive Cole, especially if he gave a good reason, but she knew in her heart that a part of her would no longer be able to fully trust him. She'd always wonder if there were other secrets he was hiding. No, she didn't envy Maisey at all.

***

Grace paced back and forth across the driveway in front of the farmhouse. Granny and Gladys had left for a walk over thirty minutes ago, and not only had they not returned, she couldn't find them anywhere. Considering both women needed assistance walking and moved at a snail's pace, their disappearance was more than a little cause for concern. It didn't seem possible for them to venture out into one of the muddy pastures, but with nowhere left to look, she had no choice but to check. She just wished she could get the images of one, or both, of them lying hurt somewhere and unable to call for help out of her head.

The sound of a car coming down the lane momentarily distracted her, and she waited to see who it was. Cole got few visitors, and Grace wasn't expecting anyone. When the car pulled up beside her, she groaned when she saw that it was the last person she wanted to see: Hunter. Okay, second to the last person. It would have been worse had it been Cole's ex-wife Valerie, but only slightly.

He got out of the car. "We need to talk," he said sternly as if he expected resistance.

"Not now," Grace shot back. "I need to find Granny, and honestly, I don't care what you have to say."

She marched to the barn where Cole kept his farm vehicles, praying one of them was available. It didn't seem likely that Granny and Gladys could have gotten far, but if they were hurt or unable to continue walking, she would need a way to transport them back to the house. When she reached the building, she breathed a huge sigh of relief when she spotted the 'mule,' which was basically a golf cart for farmers.

To her extreme annoyance, Hunter had followed her to the barn and hopped in the other side before she could drive off and leave him behind.

"I can help." He shrugged when she shot him a look.

"That's what I have a fiancé for," she retorted. "Speaking of which, this is his home. How did you even know to look for me here?"

"I went by the B&B, but you obviously weren't there. Some guy named Jim was, however, and he told me where to go. Sorry about your house," he said sincerely.

Grace shot him another dirty look. She didn't like it when he was nice; it reminded her of the Hunter she'd met at Christmas. The one who had been so kind, supportive, and charming. The one she'd so foolishly and naively believed she'd marry and grow old with. Was it possible for that Hunter to exist alongside the one who lied, cheated, and manipulated people? Humans are complicated.

They drove in silence, each on the lookout for two crazy, elderly women who had no business out here in the cow pasture. She was about to give up and return home when Hunter pointed toward the corner of the field.

"Look over there," he said, motioning, "I think that's them."

She turned the wheel and sped toward them as fast as she dared. When she pulled up to them, the sight before her was so preposterous she wasn't sure whether to laugh or cry. Simply put, Granny, Gladys, and one of Cole's cows were stuck in a mud hole, the mud just above their waists.

"What on earth!" she exclaimed. "How did this happen?"

Gladys had the decency to look chagrined, while Granny, on the other hand, looked defiant.

"We were out for our walk when we heard what sounded like an animal in distress," Granny explained. "So, being the compassionate women we are, we investigated and found Bessie here stuck in this interminable mud."

"And instead of calling Cole, you decided to jump in the mud with her?" asked Grace. "Why?"

"After Cole's misadventure the other day, Granny and I watched a video on what to do should we ever come across this situation ourselves," said Gladys. "Unfortunately, it wasn't as easy as they made it seem."

Grace looked over at Hunter and burst out laughing. The look on his face was almost as funny as the situation before her. When she was finally able to control herself again, she looked to him for help.

"Can you help me get them out of there, please?"

"I thought you didn't want my help?" he joked. When he saw her expression change, he was quick to add, "I'm just joking. What do we do?"

"If you can hold onto me, I'll reach over and grab Gladys's arms since she's closest to the edge. Gladys will grab onto Granny, and we'll pull them out."

"Sort of like a human chain?" Hunter asked as he assessed the plan.

"Yes, do you think it will work?"

It was not the best plan in the world, but it was all she could come up with on short notice. She could call Cole, but she really didn't want to explain how this happened or, more importantly, why Hunter was there if she didn't have to. She had planned to tell him about Hunter that morning, but she had overslept, and he was gone before she got up.

"I can't come up with an alternative," he shrugged. "Might as well give it a try."

Grace carefully navigated the uneven terrain to the pit's edge, her boots sinking slightly into the soft earth with each step. With a determined expression, she extended one hand towards Hunter, and the other toward Gladys. Gladys reached out eagerly, her weathered hands intertwining with Grace's firm grasp, and Granny's fragile grip.

The scene unfolded like a precarious dance as Hunter and Grace began to pull. The group strained against the resistance of the mud, their muscles flexing, as they grunted in unison. Initially, there was a glimmer of hope as they inched backward together. However, the ground beneath Grace betrayed her, causing her to slip uncontrollably into the gaping maw of mud.

With a startled gasp, Grace cascaded downwards into the viscous sludge. In the space of a heartbeat, all four figures found themselves ensnared by the unforgiving embrace of the mud pit, their bodies immobilized in its clammy grasp.

"Great!" Grace exclaimed in frustration. "What are we going to do now?"

Hunter tried in vain to pull himself out of the mud. When his failure became apparent, he threw up his hands. "I have no idea," he said through gritted teeth. "How am I supposed to explain this to Maisey?" he asked, moving his hand to indicate his mud-covered clothes.

Grace rolled her eyes, "We're stuck in a mud hole, and all you care about is the next lie you're going to tell your girlfriend?" she asked in disgust.

"My relationship with Maisey is none of your business," he shot back.

"Then stop making it my business," she shouted. "You're the one who chose to bring her to my town to stay at my hotel, and you're the one trespassing on my fiance's land in an attempt to talk me into continuing to lie to your girlfriend. If for just once in your life you would tell the truth, you wouldn't have these problems!"

"Oh yeah, miss goody-two-shoes," he snarked. "And did you go running to tell the cowboy I'm here?" he watched her expression change from anger to concern. "That's what I thought; I'm not the only liar in this pit."

Comparing her to him was a bridge too far. She did her best to maneuver through the mud so that she was close enough to slap the smug look off his face. "First of all," she said, poking her finger in his chest, "I didn't tell Cole about you because I didn't want to waste the precious time I have with him on something as insignificant as you. And second of all," she poked his chest again, "stop calling him 'the cowboy'. He's a real person with a real name, not some character in a video game."

"Children," Granny said sharply, her tone brokering no room for disobedience. "Stop this fighting at once!"

"Sorry, Granny," they said in unison.

Grace busied herself by looking around for something to grab to pull herself out of the pit. She'd just about given up when Cole and Riley pulled up in one of the other mules.

Riley, bless him, immediately burst out laughing, while Cole appeared to run the gamut of emotions, starting with anger and ending with bemusement. "Do I even want to know?" he asked Grace.

Too embarrassed to speak, she simply shook her head.

Cole nodded, "I figured as much."

When he put the mule in reverse and began to drive away, Grace feared she'd pushed him too far, and he was about to leave them there. But then he turned around, reversed a second time, and drove the mule backward to the edge of the pit. Cole and Riley exited, grabbed a chain out of the back of the bed, and handed it to Grace.

"We're going to pull you out one at a time," Cole explained. "Hold onto the chain while Riley drives forward. I'll grab you as soon as you're close enough for me to safely do so. Got it?" he asked the four of them.

They nodded in unison, then helped Granny to the chain so she could be pulled out first. Then it was Gladys's turn, then Grace, and finally Hunter. Once they were all safely out of harm's way, Cole and Riley helped Bessie out, and the adventure was finally over. Well, almost over. Grace had a feeling Cole would want a detailed explanation sooner rather than later.

"Riley, can you please take Gladys and Hunter back to the house?" Cole asked his friend and worker. "I'll bring Grace and Granny in the other mule."

"Sure thing," Riley saluted. "I wouldn't want to be you," he teased Grace on the way to the mule.

"I don't want to be me, either," she replied.

Cole helped Granny into the front of the mule, then turned to Grace, pulling her a ways away so Granny couldn't hear them. "You could have been killed," he said, his jaw working overtime to control his anger. "That cow could have rolled over at any minute, fallen on top of you, and suffocated you in the mud."

"That could have happened to any of us," she replied. "When I arrived, Granny and Gladys were already in there; what was I supposed to do?"

"Did it ever cross your mind to call me?" he asked, hurt evident in his voice. He held up his hand before she could answer. "Never mind, we can have this conversation later."

Grace followed him to the vehicle and climbed into the back. She'd messed up, and she knew it. Was she more like Hunter than she wanted to believe?

Days till Thanksgiving

-Three-

Today was the football game outing, and Grace found herself at the hotel early to prepare for the tailgating party she was throwing for her guests. Everyone knew the line to get into the parking lot at Arrowhead Stadium could stretch for miles on game day, so it was best to show up early and plan to stay late. Besides that, what's more 'American' than tailgating?

Luckily, this was Grant's big idea, so all she had to do was prepare the food and drinks and provide plenty of chairs, blankets, and sun hats to ensure her guest's comfort over the coming hours. She was also on kid duty since Aidan, Caden, and Eliza were all too young to enjoy this sort of thing, and Grace wanted their parents to have fun without the stress of dealing with bored kids. But that part she could handle. Eliza slept most of the time, and there were plenty of activities to keep the boys entertained.

Although, if she were honest, she was also looking for an excuse to avoid being at Cole's. They'd 'sort of' made up yesterday evening, but things were still tense, and she hated it. Cole had claimed to understand why she didn't immediately tell him about Hunter, but he was hurt, and she knew it. She had to find a way to make it up to him; she just hadn't come up with one yet.

As she rounded the corner to the kitchen, she stumbled across Amelia and Hugh, who were locked in an embrace. She tried to retrace her steps before they saw her, but in her haste, she stumbled and bumped into the wall. The two lovebirds heard the commotion and jerked apart like two teenagers caught making out between classes. They were momentarily relieved when they saw it was Grace, but that relief was short-lived.

Amelia rushed forward and grabbed Grace's hands. "Please don't tell anyone," she begged. "The kids aren't ready to accept our relationship, and I can't bear the thought of them hating us."

This new development explained a few things, namely why Amelia was here and willing to support her son lying to his girlfriend. Was Hunter right? Did everyone lie to suit their needs? She tried to examine her reasons for not telling Cole right away that Hunter was there. It wasn't because she still had unresolved feelings for Hunter or was afraid of Cole's reaction. She simply just didn't want to deal with it. Yes, the growing season was over, and Cole did have more time these days, but he was still busy. She much preferred to spend the time they did have together on more pleasant things than old boyfriends and their nonsense.

"I'm not going to say anything," Grace assured her, "but I really think you should. Your family is going to be more upset if they find out you're sneaking around than if you were honest with them."

"You don't understand," Amelia argued. "It's only been a couple of months since I divorced Hunter's father, and Hugh's wife just passed a year ago. They've made it clear they think it's too soon for us to find love again."

Hugh stepped forward and wrapped his arm around Amelia's shoulders. "I'm sorry to put you in this situation, lassie, but it's only for a short time. We'll tell them all about us after the holidays."

"If I was able to discover your relationship on day two of your stay here, it's only a matter of time before one of them discovers it as well," she warned. "I really think you're making a mistake, but it's your mistake to make, so you have my word that I will stay out of this."

"Thank ye," Hugh nodded. "Family relationships are complicated, but I suppose you already know that."

Grace looked from Amelia to Hugh as realization dawned on her. Hugh knew about Hunter and was choosing to remain silent, likely due to his relationship with Amelia. This had bad idea written all over it, and if they weren't careful, this trip could turn into The War of the Roses. For Grace's sake, she hoped that didn't happen. She had her own relationship problems and didn't have time to referee someone else's. But that was selfish of her. Just because she didn't like Hunter didn't mean she shouldn't help if she could.

"Enjoy the game," Grace said lamely. "The football game," she added in case they thought she was being facetious.

"Thank ye," they replied in unison.

Grace smiled to herself as she continued to the kitchen. It was nice to see Amelia happy. She knew Amelia's first marriage had been more of a business deal than a love affair, and she was excited to see that Amelia had found someone to love her for simply being her. Everyone should get to have that experience at least once in their lives.

At two o'clock sharp, Grant pulled the bus up out back and helped her load all the food she'd prepared. The plan was for him to grill burgers, bratwursts, and corn on the cob and serve beans, chips, and cole slaw on the side. For dessert, Grace had included brownies, an assortment of cookies, and a couple of loaves of banana bread. She'd be shocked if they managed to go through all the food, but the stadium sold plenty of beer and nachos if they did.

"Have fun!" Grace called out as soon as everyone was seated on the bus.

Molly came rushing over to give Eliza one last kiss goodbye. "Are you sure you're okay with this?" she asked. "I can always stay home."

"It's fine," Grace assured her. "If I have any problems, I'll call Gladys, okay?"

The torn look on her face broke Grace's heart. Molly loved her daughter and didn't want to leave her, but she wanted to have a life too. Was this how all new moms felt? Grace tried to imagine herself with a baby and could definitely understand where Molly was coming from.

"Okay," Molly said reluctantly. "You can always call me, too," she reminded her. "I'll take an Uber home if I have to."

"Molly," Grant called out to his wife. "Get on the bus, Eliza is in safe hands."

Grace waved a second time, then took the boys and Eliza inside.

"What do you want to do first?" she asked Aidan and Caden. "We have board games, painting supplies, movies, video games..." she trailed off as they took off running ahead of her. When she reached the dining room, she found them eagerly going through her stack of games.

Before long, the brothers began to fight, and Eliza began to cry. This was going to be a long night.

***

It took almost two hours to get all the kids to sleep, but she finally did it. Peace and quiet had never felt so rewarding, but after seven hours of non-stop chaos, she felt she'd certainly earned it. Next time, she would have to remember to get permission to take the kids to the park to play.

Worn out and exhausted, she sat down on one of the chairs in the lobby. The door to the boy's room was open so she could hear them if they called out. With little Eliza fast asleep in her playpen, Grace could finally take a break.

When the little bell on the entrance door jingled, she practically screamed, fearing it would wake someone. As soon as she saw it was Cole, she calmed down and tried to relax once more. Too bad she was now so wound up at the sight of him; relaxation had become an impossibility.

"What are you doing here?" she asked softly.

He sat beside her and reached out to grab her hand. "Now that we've had time to think things through, we should talk."

Grace nodded, her old familiar fears taking hold. Would she ever get over them? Losing her parents at such a young age seemed to have given her some deep-seated abandonment issues. Whenever she and Cole disagreed, she became convinced he would leave her. It wasn't healthy; she should probably see someone about that at some point.

Cole took a deep breath and let it out slowly. "I just want to know why you chose not to tell me about Hunter?"

She could tell he'd left out part of his question, which she suspected was: did she still have feelings for Hunter?

"When Molly first told us about our guests, Rebekah and I suspected Hunter was involved when we heard they were from Scotland. It just seemed like too much of a coincidence, you know?" she asked without expecting an answer. "But it also seemed a little silly to speculate on something that could turn out not to be true. So, I let it go and moved forward with our plans."

"That's interesting to hear," he said slowly. "So, what you're saying is it wasn't a surprise when he showed up?"

Once again, he sounded hurt, as if she'd been keeping this from him.

"No," she quickly assured him. "I mean, yes, I was still surprised. It was crazy for him to come back here after all this time. I had no reason to suspect he would actually do so."

"This leads back to my original question, then," he said. "Why didn't you tell me?"

"Because I didn't care," she stated matter-of-factly. "The biggest theme throughout our whole relationship has been lack of time together," she explained. "I could have told you Saturday night, should have told you, but then we would have wasted precious minutes talking about him. Minutes we should have spent on us." She sighed, her head in her hands. "I planned to tell you Sunday morning, but then I overslept, and well, you know the rest."

Cole pulled her into his lap and turned her face up to look at him. "I understand, I just don't like feeling there are secrets between us, darlin'. Trust and communication are the two most important aspects of a healthy relationship."

"I promise I wasn't trying to keep it a secret, and if Hunter shows up again in the future, you'll be the first to know. But I really hope that never happens."

He responded by kissing her, gently at first, before deepening it as much as he dared considering where they were. When he pulled back, he looked deep into her eyes. "I will never forget seeing you in that mud hole," he deadpanned. "As soon as I got over the shock, I have to admit it was one of the funniest things I've ever seen. The looks on all your faces were absolutely hysterical. Riley and I must have laughed about it for a solid minute!"

Grace playfully smacked his arm and rolled her eyes. "It couldn't have been any funnier than when you fell in the mud the other day," she teased.

"Luckily, you'll never know. Seriously, though, if this ever happens again, and Lord do I pray it never does, please call me. I'm still hurt that you chose not to."

"The only reason I didn't call is I honestly thought we could get them out on our own. I had no idea how dangerous it was. It was stupidity on my part, not because I was trying to hide Hunter from you," she explained.

"You never told me why he was there in the first place."

Eliza began to fuss, and Grace leaned over to check on her. When she stopped and resumed sleeping, Grace turned back to Cole and explained Hunter's current situation.

"So, basically, he wants you to lie for him?"

"That about sums it up," Grace replied.

"I don't like the sound of that," Cole said, his brow furrowed. "What are you going to do?"

Grace shook her head. "Nothing. I refuse to lie, but I won't volunteer information either. I have a feeling this will all come to a head naturally, so all I can do at this point is try to be the best host I can be."

"I guess that makes sense. Maybe the tree falling on your house is a blessing in disguise. Imagine if all this were taking place at the B&B instead."

"I don't have to imagine; I already lived it, remember?"

He gently ran his fingers down the side of her face then brushed his thumb against her lips. "How could I forget? I think I still owe Hunter that debt of gratitude. If he hadn't messed up so bad, I might have missed my chance with you."

"I refuse to believe that," she whispered. She was transfixed by the blue of his eyes gazing into hers. "We were always meant to be together; nothing could have changed that."

Cole kissed her again then gently set her back in her chair. "If I don't leave now, I may not be able to."

It was tempting to wrap her arms around his legs to stop him from leaving, but she managed to refrain. The guests would be back soon, and getting caught in the lobby with her fiance would not be a good look. So she waited it out like a grown-up, counting down the minutes until she could go home and see him again.

Days till Thanksgiving

-Two-

Two days till Thanksgiving, and Grace couldn't wait until the big day. She was currently in the hotel kitchen making up a big batch of tarts for that night's dessert when she heard a commotion:

"HOW COULD YE," screamed Maisey. "YOU'RE NOTHING BUT A LIAR AND A CHEAT!"

Grace's eyes widened, and she immediately took off toward the sound of the screams, coming to a screeching halt when she reached the lobby, where she found Hunter, Maisey, and Rebekah.

Rebekah looked at Grace and held up her hands. "I know what this looks like, but it wasn't me."

Grace's heart went out to Maisey when she saw the tears streaming down her face. "What's wrong?" she asked Maisey, though she suspected she already knew the answer.

"What's wrong is I discovered Hunter and Rebekah have a thing together, and he never told me." She shook her head in disgust. "All those times I talked about her, and ye said NOTHING!"

"Had a thing," Rebekah corrected. "Hunter and I haven't been together in a long time."

"Is that supposed to make me feel better?" she asked angrily. "What else are ye hiding from me?" she demanded to know. "Did ye have a thing with the innkeeper as well?"

Grace stepped back and did her best to keep her expression neutral, but it didn't matter; Hunter gave it away.

"It's not what you think," he said lamely. He looked to Grace for help, "Please tell her," he begged.

"Hunter and I had a brief fling last Christmas that was over almost as quickly as it began," Grace explained. "It meant nothing to either of us, and I can assure you I have moved on," she held out her hand so Maisey could see her engagement ring.

Hunter shot Grace a pained look but wisely chose to remain silent.

"If that's true, why didn't Hunter tell me about ye?" Maisey demanded to know.

"Look, I have nothing to do with that," Grace said, moving closer to the door. "But I'm sure Hunter has his reasons."

Maisey stamped her foot in frustration. "I've been honest with ye from day one," she told Hunter. "All I asked in return was for ye to be honest with me. I don't understand why ye chose to lie about something so insignificant."

"I doubt it's the only lie he told," Rebekah snarked.

Grace shot Rebekah a look and shook her head. This was going to get ugly fast.

"What's going on in here?" cried Hugh as he entered the room.

"Hunter lied to me, Da," Maisey explained.

The rest of the family, stirred up by the commotion, followed Hugh into the room.

Hunter ran his hand through his hair and sighed. "Look, I didn't lie; I just chose not to tell you about certain parts of my life I was ashamed of, okay," he tried to take Maisey's hands in his, but she yanked them back. "Maisey, please," he begged. "Just give me a chance to explain."

"I think ye've done enough, son," Hugh said, wrapping his arm around Maisey's shoulders.

Logan snorted his attention squarely on his dad. "How is this any different than ye lying about dating Hunter's ma?" he asked.

An audible gasp sounded from the group, as each turned to look at Hugh.

"Is that true?" Brianna asked her dad.

At the same time, Hunter turned to his mom, "You're dating Maisey's father?"

He shook his head in disbelief. "This is insane," he said more to himself than anyone else. He turned back to Maisey and sighed. "Look, I'm sorry; I never should have kept the truth from you, but I didn't do it to hurt you; I did it because I knew if you knew the real me, you'd realize what a scumbag I am, and you'd never give me the time of day."

He paused to take a breath, then continued. "I worked really hard to move on from my past. I moved to a new country, I got a new job, new friends, and a new girlfriend.

All I wanted to do was put as much distance between me and the man I was as possible."

"It doesn't sound like ye learned from yer past mistakes," said Maisey. "It sounds like ye tried to outrun them, and failed. Ye should have trusted me enough to share yer secrets with me. I may have surprised ye."

She whipped around to face her father. "Ye should have done the same," she said, shaking her finger at him. "All we ever wanted was for ye to be happy, and now look at us; we're all miserable."

Maisey burst into tears and ran from the room. Hunter stormed through the exit with Amelia close behind. The rest of the family went to their separate rooms, and a chorus of slamming doors followed.

Grace looked at Rebekah and raised a brow. "Should I call Kenzie and cancel the wine tasting?"

Rebekah shook her head. "I'd give it some time; they might decide they could use a drink or two after that showdown."

"That's fair," Grace nodded. "Think we should go have a talk with Maisey?"

"I feel like we might be the last people she wants to see right now, but let's go anyway. We'll give her an invitation to the I Hate Hunter Club," Rebekah joked.

"The way things are going, she might dethrone you as the sitting president!"

Rebekah snorted. "She wishes. Compared to mere minutes for her, I have years of grievances against that man."

They found Maisey in the kitchen, crying at the table in the corner. On the way over there, Grace grabbed a tray of her yummy cranberry, walnut, and brie crackers, and set them down in front of Maisey.

"You're going to love these," Rebekah said, popping one in her mouth. She pushed the tray toward Maisey. "Try a couple," she prodded. "And before you know it, you'll have forgotten all about what's-his-name,"

Maisey chuckled and did as she was told. "These are yummy," she agreed in surprise.

The tray was empty in no time, and Maisey's tears were dry.

"How did you find out about me and Hunter?" Rebekah asked.

"I was bored, so I decided to scroll through social media and stumbled upon an old picture of the two of ye. I don't know how I missed it before...." she trailed off, her cheeks reddening from embarrassment. "I'm still excited to meet ye," she told Rebekah. "I've been a fan for years."

"If you've been following me that long, I'm surprised this is the first you've seen us. Hunter's been a part of my posts off and on from the very beginning. To be fair, I did erase him from my accounts once we broke up for good."

Grace remembered her time with Hunter and was sure she knew the problem. "Hunter always tries to hide his face," she explained to the two of them. "I remember trying to take pictures of him for his memory book last Christmas, and he would either turn away or pull the brim of his hat down low. It was such an annoyance at the time, but it makes sense now, I guess."

"You make him sound like he's in witness protection," Rebekah joked. "In all honesty, though, he worried about it a lot. Since he had a job on Wall Street, he had to be super careful to protect his image, so he didn't get in trouble with the big bosses. Daddy's name and money will only get you so far in that crowd."

Maisey's head shot up. "What do ye mean? I thought his da was dead?"

Rebekah pursed her lips. "I would love nothing more than to give you the dirt on all things Hunter, but I think you need to give him the opportunity to do it himself. Then you can decide if giving him a second chance is worth it."

"If you were in my shoes, would you give him another chance?" she asked Grace and Rebekah.

"Hunter and I go all the way back to when we were in diapers," Rebekah explained. "So I can't give you an unbiased answer. If I were to have this same issue with my current boyfriend, I think the answer would depend on what he has to say and whether or not I felt I could trust him going forward. Only you can make that decision."

They both looked to Grace for her opinion. "It's easy to picture Hunter in my mind and say no," Grace reasoned out. "But if I picture Cole, then my perspective changes. I love him too much to throw it all away without at least giving him a chance to explain himself."

"Do ye know where he might have gone?" Maisey asked.

Her mind appeared to be made up, and Grace truly wished her the best of luck. It was going to be a difficult conversation, and she didn't envy her one bit. But maybe this was exactly what they needed.

"I'm right here," Hunter said from the doorway. "I was actually coming to say goodbye. Mom and I have decided to return to Scotland early so we don't ruin the rest of your trip."

"Ach, yer the reason we're on this trip in the first place," Maisey reminded him. "A bit cheeky of ye to be runnin' off like that and leavin' us behind."

Grace needed her kitchen back so she could get started on lunch. "Why don't you two talk in the dining room, where it's private? We can close the doors and make sure no one disturbs you." She checked her watch and saw there were only a couple of hours till lunch. Hopefully, they'd be finished by then.

"We can go to my room," said Maisey. "That way, we don't get it yer way."

Once they were safely out of earshot, Grace breathed a sigh of relief. "That went better than expected."

"Now what are we going to do about the rest of them?" asked Rebekah. "I'm not sure that's going to be as easy to smooth over."

"Bold of you to assume this one will end well," Grace retorted. "We're putting a lot of stock in Maisey's willingness to forgive."

"She's at least willing to try," Rebekah mused. "I'm not so sure the others will be."

Grace mulled that one over. It was hard to imagine how her guests felt when she lacked their experience, but most children wanted their parents to be happy, right? Maybe they could play up that angle and see how it went. "Should we take them to the winery first?"

Rebekah raised a brow. "Are you trying to get them drunk first? Grace, I would never have expected such a thing from you!"

"Look, desperate times call for desperate measures. We can't have our guests warring over the holidays."

"Why not? We promised them an authentic American Thanksgiving, didn't we?" she deadpanned.

Grace tried to hide her smile but couldn't. "I don't think that's what they meant by authentic," she laughed.

Rebekah joined in her laughter. "We'll try it your way, first," she replied. "I'll even go with you to help referee."

"You just don't want to miss out on the drama," Grace accused.

"You're darn right!" she exclaimed. "This is the most exciting thing to happen in weeks. I've got to get my entertainment where I can."

Grace elbowed Rebekah and laughed. "You're terrible!"

"Eh, aren't we all."

Days till Thanksgiving

-One-

The trip to the winery had been a failure. The once rambunctious group had primarily remained silent until a screaming match between Hugh, Logan, and Brianna broke out. Maxwell had taken the boys outside while Rebekah and Grace tried to quell the fight. When that failed and glasses started flying, security stepped in and escorted them all out.

Luckily, Wyatt and Kenzie, the winery owners, had agreed not to press charges if the family agreed to pay for damages. Despite that, Grace had a feeling she wouldn't be welcomed back with open arms anytime soon.

When they arrived back at the hotel, they discovered Hunter and Maisey had not fared any better. Maisey had been so angered by Hunter's confession she'd kicked him out and then locked herself in her room and refused to come out.

But that was yesterday. Today was the community football game, and Grace was so determined to make her guests have fun that she would hogtie them and drag them there by their shoelaces if she had to. Besides that, nothing healed family wounds like a good old-fashioned friendly competition, right? Right?

Since she wasn't sure they would listen to her, despite her previous threats, when it was time to go, Grace sent in the big guns. And by big guns, she meant Molly. No one said no to Molly; it just wasn't done. So Grace left her guests in Molly's capable hands and left early to make sure the park was set up and everything was in place.

When she arrived, she was thrilled to see everything was already set up and in place. Food trailers lined the edge of the parking lot, offering a variety of foods and drinks ranging from hot cocoa and cider to tacos, barbecue sandwiches, and pizza. There was even a sign for funnel cakes and cotton candy. No one can stay in a bad mood after eating a funnel cake.

Since the vendors had everything under control, she made her way over to the makeshift field and saw the bleachers were in place and already filled with spectators. If this went well, she could see this becoming a regular community event, and she loved that for her town.

She spent some time chatting with some of her neighbors before spotting the bus Molly had rented for her guests. By the looks of it, Molly had succeeded in getting everyone here, and Grace couldn't be more grateful.

"Coming here was the biggest mistake of my life," Hunter spat at her as he stomped by.

"Then why did you?" she called after him.

He spun on his heel and stomped back to her. "It wasn't my choice," he said through gritted teeth. Maisey booked this whole trip as a surprise, and I should have found a way to decline the second I realized where we were headed."

"Again, why didn't you? Come on, Hunter, you couldn't have believed you could come back to a town this size, and no one would claim to know you. Be honest; you came here because you wanted to get caught."

"Why would I want that?" he sputtered. "It makes no sense. You're making no sense."

"It's simple," she said, placing a comforting hand on his shaking arm. "You were tired of living a lie."

Hunter shook his head, unable to process her words. "I can't do this right now," he said, taking a shaky breath.

Grace let go and stepped back, giving him room to breathe. "If you need to talk, I'll listen," she assured him.

Maisey passed by them, and if looks could kill, they'd both be dead. Grace was glad she was merely a spectator because you couldn't pay her enough to take the field with a woman out for blood. And from the looks of things, she wasn't the only Campbell with an axe to grind. Grace briefly wondered if she should warn the coaches but decided as high school teachers, they likely had plenty of experience with this kind of thing.

Hugh and Amelia walked over, and judging by their body language, they were just as dejected as Hunter and Maisey.

"I'm sorry about yesterday," Grace said to them. "I'd hoped things would improve with a trip to the winery."

"You warned us," said Amelia. "We should have listened to you and talked to the kids. Now it's too late." Tears stung her eyes, threatening to spill over onto her cheeks. "They'll never accept me now," she said sadly.

Hugh put his arm around her and pulled her close. "There, there, dinna fash, my love. They'll come around. We just need to give them time."

Amelia's hands covered her face as she leaned against Hugh's chest. "You don't know that."

Maxwell walked up, his sons in tow. "Everything okay?" he asked when he saw Amelia's face.

When they didn't immediately respond, Grace felt compelled to break the awkward silence. "Amelia's upset about...you know."

"Ach, yes. I should have known that," he nodded. "Don't worry, Amelia, Brianna's all aflame now, but once she calms down, she'll see reason again."

"Do you really think so?" Amelia asked hopefully.

"I do," he replied confidently. "Would ye be willing to sit with the boys while we play? They're a little young for this, and I don't want them left unattended."

Amelia's face lit up at the request. "I'd be happy to watch them. Do you mind if I take them to get lunch before the game starts?"

The boys perked up at the mention of food. "Please, da," they said in unison.

Maxwell laughed and rolled his eyes. "Ye'd think we never feed the lads!" He shook his head and addressed his sons. "Now ye be good for Amelia. No rough-housing."

"We promise," Aidan said. He nudged his younger with his elbow, and Caden nodded emphatically.

Hugh and Maxwell continued toward the field while Amelia and the boys walked in the opposite direction to the food trailers. Grace looked around and saw Logan sitting by himself on one of the park benches. His headphones were firmly in place, as was the sullen look she'd seen him with since they arrived. However, Grace suspected a lot more was going on beneath the surface than he let on.

"Is this seat taken?" she asked, sitting next to him before he replied. She tapped him on the shoulder to get his attention when he remained silent.

He looked over and appeared surprised to see she was there. "Did ye need something?" he asked, removing his headphones.

"I was about to ask you the same thing," she replied. "Are you okay?"

Logan shrugged. "Everything's fine."

Grace nodded. "Of course it is. You're in a foreign country far from home, your entire family is fighting with one another, and you're stuck in the middle with nowhere to go and no one to talk to. Sounds like things are great to me!"

He snorted, a hint of a smile appearing on his lips. "When ye say it like that, I guess things aren't so great."

"Want to talk about it? I've been told I'm a pretty good listener."

"It's my fault they're all fighting," he sighed. "I shouldn't have said anything, I was just so upset about all the lying. We came over here like one big happy family, yet everyone was hiding all these secrets. I couldn't take it anymore."

This was a difficult situation, and Grace needed to tread lightly lest she inadvertently make things worse. "It's not your fault," she said gently. "I don't believe anyone acted out of malice or deceit, they just didn't know how to communicate without fear of hurting someone, so they chose to remain silent instead."

"But does that really make it okay?"

"No, I'm not excusing their behavior, I'm just trying to explain it. Adults make mistakes, too, you know." She lightly bumped his shoulder with hers. "The important part is to own your mistake and do what you can to make it right."

"I don't feel Da and Amelia have tried to make things right. Maybe that's what's missing from all this."

Grace patted his arm. "I'm sure they'll apologize as soon as everyone is ready to receive it. I can tell you this, Amelia cares a lot for your family. She's devastated over the rift and desperately wants to make things right."

"I care for Amelia, too," he admitted sheepishly. "I don't mind her seeing me Da, I just wish they would be honest about it."

"I agree. Now, why don't you join the others on the field? It looks like the game is about to start, and you don't want to miss an opportunity to spend time with your family. Even if they are at war," she joked.

Logan put his headphones back on and stood. "Thanks, Grace," he called over his shoulder as he headed toward the field.

She watched him go. He was tall, like his father, but still in the lanky teenage phase, with a smattering of acne across his chin and forehead. His hair was a strawberry blonde, his eyes an emerald green. He was the complete opposite of his sisters, Maisey and Brianna. She couldn't help but wonder what their mother had looked like.

At this point, it was time for the game to start, so Grace joined Amelia and the boys in the stands. Hunter sat one row below them, his attention on his phone.

"Get on the field, ye coward," screamed Maisey. She walked over, yanked the phone out of his hand, then ran back to her side of the fifty-yard line.

It looked like Hunter was going to ignore Maisey's taunts when Amelia nudged him and nodded toward the field. He may have been willing to ignore his girlfriend, but he wasn't willing to ignore his mom. Pretty soon, everyone was on a team and ready to go.

Excitement hung in the chilly air as everyone waited for the game to start. Everywhere she looked, she saw cups of hot cocoa, brightly colored hats and scarves, and plenty of homemade signs with names printed boldly in permanent markers. This was going to be fun, and Grace didn't even like football.

The coaches quickly divided the teams, and from where Grace sat, it looked like Maisey and Hugh were on one team, and Hunter, Brianna, Logan, and Maxwell were on another. Jim and Coach Bryant also appeared to be on opposing teams. Which was odd, since Coach Bryant had claimed he'd be too busy to be here today.

When she looked again, the Campbell family was sporting war paint, and Grace was now concerned. Did she need to remind everyone this was supposed to be flag football? And that it was supposed to be fun? They didn't look like they were here for fun; they looked like they were about to re-enact a scene from Braveheart. Even Logan had shed his headphones and sullen demeanor in exchange for a battle cry and fist pumps.

The whistle blew, and everyone took their places. A coin was flipped, and Hugh and Maisey's team were announced winners. Grace leaned forward in her seat, her anxiety running wild. A second whistle blew, the football was airborne, and then both teams rushed forward with a shout as bodies flew everywhere.

At the sound of another whistle, everyone stopped and looked around. Someone was down on the field and appeared to be injured. The crowd parted to reveal Coach Bryant on the ground, his arms wrapped around his knee.

"It was him," he shouted, pointing at Jim. "He broke my knee on purpose."

Given the number of people on the field, Grace had no idea how he could possibly know that. To her, it had looked like utter chaos. Then again, she wouldn't be surprised if he was using this as an excuse to frame Jim and make him look bad in front of the judge.

A couple of guys she didn't know helped him off the field, and then they took a five-minute break to remind everyone of the rules. When the game resumed, the no-touching rule took effect, and they spent the rest of the time chasing each other around the field.

By the time it was over, Maisey and Hugh's team were declared the winners, and everyone was still mad. Grace's hopes of a mission success had turned into mission failure. Yes, it was naive to think a football game would repair the rift in the family, but it had been worth a shot.

-Happy Thanksgiving!-

Grace slipped out of bed, careful not to wake Rebekah. She was used to getting up this early, but after the stressful week she'd had, she found she was more tired than usual. Cole was already up and dressed when she entered the kitchen. There was no such thing as a day off from work when you lived on a farm, even if it was a major holiday. Animals still had to be fed, and stalls still had to be cleaned.

She walked up behind him and wrapped her arms around his waist. "I need to go to the hotel to get the turkeys in the oven. Will I see you there later?"

"Of course," he replied, squeezing her arms. "I'll try to get there early so I can help out."

"I would love that," she replied, kissing the back of his neck. "It's been a little crazy there lately, so maybe your presence will keep everyone in check."

Cole chuckled between sips of coffee. "I feel like my presence is more likely to add to the chaos than prevent it, but I'll certainly try."

Grace sighed. "Our first Thanksgiving together," she said dreamily.

He kissed the tip of her nose, then grabbed his thermos. "You remember that when Hunter and Maisey start flinging mashed potatoes at each other, okay?"

"Good thing the hotel has insurance," she joked. "What, too soon?" she asked innocently when she saw the dark look on his face.

He shook his head and did his best to hide his smile. "I can't live without you, you know that, right?"

"Lucky for you, you'll never have to." She blew him a kiss and left, whistling on her way to her car. It would be a good day, even if she had to feed everyone in separate rooms, but she would do her best to ensure it didn't come to that.

When she arrived at the hotel, she found Aidan and Caden coloring quietly in the lobby, and she once again patted herself on the back for having the foresight to stock the cabinets with crayons and coloring books.

"Hey guys," she said to the boys. "Want to help me in the kitchen?"

They gave an enthusiastic shriek and jumped up to follow her. Once in the kitchen, she helped them wash their hands and then gave them gingerbread cookies and icing to decorate with. While they were busy doing that, she got the turkeys in the oven and then started work on the dinner rolls.

"Grace?" said Aidan. "We're hungry."

She checked her watch and saw that it was time for breakfast. "Sorry about that, guys, I lost track of time. Want to help me carry food to the dining room?"

They nodded eagerly, so she handed them a box of donuts and assorted pastries she'd bought from Bea's the day before, and a loaf of bread for toast. Oatmeal packets and cereal were already on the buffet, so all that was left was for her to scramble some eggs and fry some bacon.

While she was doing that, Brianna walked into the kitchen. "I hope the boys haven't been bothering ye," she said stiffly. "They've been chatting non-stop about all the 'help' they've been giving ye."

"They've been very helpful," Grace assured her.

"Good," she nodded, then turned to leave.

Grace had never been good at minding her business, so why start now? "Wait!" she called after Brianna. "Can we talk for a moment? Please."

Brianna took a seat on one of the stools and folded her arms across her chest. "I know me family hasn't been acting right, but this is between us."

"I know losing your mom was hard, and I'm sorry for that, but just because Hugh has started dating again doesn't mean you're going to lose him, too."

"What do ye know about loss?" she asked bitterly.

It always amazed her that people assumed they were the only ones in the world hurting. She did not relish sharing her personal tragedies with strangers, but she would do it if it would help end their suffering. "I lost both of my parents when I was a child," Grace stated. "And I almost lost my granny, the only family member I have left, last Christmas. In fact, she's the reason I started hosting these Experiences in the first place. So I imagine I know more than I've ever wished to about loss."

Brianna looked at her in horror. "Ach, I'm so sorry," she said, guilt crossing her face. "I had no idea. Ye seem to have so many friends and family around, I just assumed ye had it all."

"This time last year, there was no one but Granny and me. Well, and Gladys," Grace added. "Which is kind of my point. As soon as I opened my heart and allowed others to come in, it wasn't long before it was full to bursting."

"Ye think I should forgive me da and accept him with Amelia, don't ye?"

Grace nodded. "I really do. It's obvious you like her. Would it really be so bad if she dated your dad?"

"Ye've given me some things to think about," she replied. She stood and turned to the leave. "I need to get back to me, kids; thanks, Grace."

It wasn't a total win, but Brianna hadn't left angry, so that was a start. She went back to her preparations. The pies and appetizers were ready to be served, the rolls were proofing, and the turkeys were in the oven. That just left...everything else. But she could do this. She would do this. Her guests were counting on her to provide a memorable meal, and she would do everything possible to make it happen. She just hoped it was memorable for all the right reasons.

***

While Grace cooked, Cole, Rebekah, and Thorne rearranged the tables in the dining room to create one long table to seat everyone. Since the family was still at war, it was a bit of a risk, but she couldn't stand the thought of everyone sitting at separate tables for a holiday meal.

Linda had come through with a couple of gorgeous and festive centerpieces bursting with Autumn flowers and glistening berries. Grace had decided to throw caution to the wind by adding candles to the mix to create a more intimate setting and ambiance. The delicate dance of light and shadow created an enchanting atmosphere, transforming the dining table into a scene straight out of a luxurious home decor magazine. In her humble opinion, of course.

Since there were so many people, she decided to serve buffet-style rather than try to cram all the dishes onto the table. It had seemed like a good idea, but now that she was watching everyone file through the line, she felt it was giving off 'cafeteria' vibes and wished she had come up with a different idea. Oh well, nothing she could do about it now.

She was about to take out the last dish when Hunter appeared in the kitchen.

"Why do I keep messing things up?" he asked sadly. "It feels like every time I get it right, it ends up being so wrong."

Grace set the dish on the counter and gave him her full attention. "When you spend your life living for others, it becomes hard to live for yourself. You're so busy trying to be who they want you to be you lose who you truly are."

"I was convinced that if I left my past here in the States, I could start fresh somewhere new. Why was that so wrong? Am I really the bad guy for wanting that?"

She reached across the counter and took his hand. "You're not the bad guy for that. Just like you wouldn't have been the bad guy for breaking up with me after you left last Christmas. The problem is that you choose to lie to avoid uncomfortable and difficult conversations."

"I don't mean to," he sighed and ran a hand over his face.

"I know," she said softly. "You're so afraid to let people see the real you that you sabotage your relationships before anyone can get too close. That way, no one has the opportunity to hurt you."

Confused, he shook his head. "How can you see things so clearly?"

"Because you and I are a lot alike, silly. I've been lucky enough to find someone willing to chase me when I try to run. Who sees through the pain to the hurt little girl who desperately wants to be loved. And I think you've found someone willing to do that for you, too. But you need to be brave enough to let her."

Hunter squeezed her hand in return. "Thanks, Grace. I really appreciate this."

"I'm happy to help," she replied. "Seriously, Hunter. I know I haven't shown it, but I want you to find happiness."

He nodded, then left in the direction of the dining room, leaving her alone with her thoughts. What she'd said had been true; she genuinely did want him to be happy. Life was too short to hold onto grudges.

She picked up the dish and followed him, relieved to see everyone assembled in the dining room and waiting patiently for the buffet. They weren't talking, but they weren't fighting, either, so that was a win.

Once everyone had a plate, she addressed the group. "Now that everyone is seated, would you like to take turns sharing something you're thankful for?" This had always been Granny's favorite Thanksgiving tradition, even though their meal had consisted of a frozen TV dinner with a slice of pie from Bea's Bakery for dessert.

Hunter pushed his chair back and stood. "I have something I need to say," he announced to the tale.

Sitting between Cole and Rebekah, Grace reached out and grabbed their hands. She then said a quick prayer that Hunter wasn't about to ruin Thanksgiving.

"There are a lot of people at this table that I've hurt over the years: Grace, Rebekah, Maisey," he nodded at each one as he said their name, "and myself." He bowed his head in shame for a moment, then lifted it again to face them. "It was never my intention to hurt you; in fact, I was trying to do the opposite, but in my misguided attempt to be what I thought each of you wanted me to be, I did more damage than if I had just been honest."

The group exchanged glances, unsure of what to say or do.

"Rebekah," Hunter continued, "you were my closest friend and ally. I know neither of us truly wanted to marry each other, but the way I handled that was so unfair to you. I abandoned you to face the wrath of our parents alone, and for that, I am truly sorry."

Rebekah squeezed Grace's hand and wiped her eyes with a napkin with her other hand. "Thank you, Hunter, I appreciate your apology and am willing to accept it."

"I know I don't deserve it, but thank you," he replied. He turned to Grace. "You gave me the most wonderful gift I've ever received, and I repaid you with heartache and lies. Before I met you, I was trapped in a life I hated with no hope I could ever get out. But you showed me what life could be like if I dared to free myself. You have often said that our time together meant nothing, but you're wrong, Grace; it meant everything."

Tears flowed down Grace's cheeks as she listened to words she had never allowed herself to acknowledge she needed to hear. She believed with all her heart that Cole was her soulmate, but a part of her had once believed in a life with Hunter, and it had hurt beyond belief to believe he had only been using her. "Thank you, Hunter," said Grace. "It means a lot to me to hear you say that."

"Cole, I'm sorry about the incident on the farm the other day. I was only trying to help, but it was rude of me to show up like I did."

"You're forgiven," said Cole. He squeezed Grace's hand under the table.

Grace squeezed his hand back, a subtle thank you for being the amazing man he was.

Hunter turned to Maisey. "Grace told me yesterday she believed I agreed to come here because I wanted to get caught, and she's right. I really wanted to be the man I told you I was, but I'm not. My intention was never to hurt or deceive you, I just wanted a chance to have this kind of life," he said, sweeping his arm to indicate everyone in the room. "I knew I'd never have this if I told you the truth."

"We all make mistakes, Hunter. And we all have things in our pasts we're not proud of. Maisey's voice wavered, a mix of hurt and frustration coloring her words. "Ye should've trusted me, Hunter. We're supposed to be partners." She paused, her eyes searching his face. "Sharing the weight, ye know? Not... not buildin' walls between us."

He nodded as tears streamed down both their faces. "I'm so sorry."

"In the spirit of Thanksgiving, I'm willing to give ye another chance, but Hunter, if I ever find out ye've lied to me again, I'll be shovin' ye straight into the loch—cannae say I'll bother pullin' ye oot either!"

"Fair enough," he smiled, his relief a juxtaposition to his tears. "The turkey's getting cold," he laughed. "Sorry about that, too."

After Hunter sat, Hugh stood and addressed the table. "I'm sorry to keep ye from the turkey a little longer, but this needs to be said." He grabbed Amelia's hand and motioned for her to stand beside him. "I'm not sorry for me relationship with this bonnie lass, but I am sorry for hiding it from ye. Ye deserve the truth, no matter how painful it can be at times, and from now on, I promise to be honest with ye."

Amelia, who appeared to be choked up, nodded her agreement.

"Now, let's dig into this amazing feast Grace has prepared for us!"

Brianna stood, a stern expression on her face. "Ye're free to eat," she announced, "but I, too, have something that needs to be said. After careful consideration, I have decided we were wrong to tell ye not to date," she said to Hugh. "Ye and Amelia have me blessing. That is all." She sat down and picked up her fork, and the rest of her family followed suit.

Grace wasn't sure what to do, so she picked up her fork and began to eat as well. When everyone had finished, she cleared the dinner plates and offered dessert. "Would anyone like to share something they're thankful for?" she asked, deciding to give it a second try.

"I'm thankful for second chances," said Hunter.

"I'll drink to that," said Hugh. He raised his glass in a toast, as did the rest of the table.

When no one else spoke, Grace tried again. "Anyone else?"

Grant looked around the room, then back to Grace. "I think everyone here is thankful for a second chance," he said. He gave Molly a loving look. "I know I am."

"I'm thankful for pie," Aidan said happily.

"Me, too!" Caden agreed.

When she thought about it, she realized he was right. Everyone in the room had been given a second chance at either love, life, or happiness at some point throughout the year. If that wasn't something to be thankful for, she didn't know what was.

Epilogue

It was time to say goodbye to the Campbell family and Grace found she was more sad than she'd expected to be. Once everyone had made up at Thanksgiving, they'd had a good time together, playing games, watching sports, and sharing stories over leftovers and second, and in some cases, third helpings of pie.

The day after had been more of the same, and they'd chosen to end the Experience with a trip to the city to see the Christmas lights. There was a drive-through light display everyone wanted to see, so they'd loaded up the bus, and headed out. Her guests were a lively bunch, and she'd never had so much in her life. There was already talk of them coming back next year, and she found she was already looking forward to it.

Rebekah and Grace stood in the lobby, waiting to help load their luggage. Amelia and Hugh were the first to leave.

"Goodbye, Lassies!" he said, giving them each a bear hug. "If ye ever find yerselves in Scotland, be sure to look us up!"

"We will do that," Grace laughed. Maybe someday she'd actually take him up on that offer.

Hugh grabbed their luggage and left for the car, leaving Amelia alone to say her goodbyes.

"It was good to see you again, Amelia," Grace said, giving her a hug. "I'm so glad you were able to find your happily-ever-after."

Amelia hugged her back, then hugged Rebekah. "Every time I come here my life seems to improve dramatically," she said sentimentally. "It's like there's magic in the air, or something."

Grace smiled, "We provide the location, our guests provide the magic."

"No darling," Amelia shook her head. "It's you. You're the one that provides the magic. Speaking of which, thank you for speaking to Brianna. She changed her mind because of what you said. I will never forget that."

"I was happy to help."

Amelia took one last look around, then nodded to herself. "Goodbye, girls, take care of yourselves."

"She's really changed," Rebekah said softly. "I wish my mom would."

Grace out her arm around Rebekah and squeezed her shoulders. "I'm sorry," she replied gently. "Maybe some day she'll surprise you."

Rebekah laid her head on Grace's shoulder. "It's a nice thought, but I'm not going to hold my breath."

Hunter and Maisey were next to leave, each dragging their suitcase behind them. "I'm not good at goodbyes," said Maisey. "So, I'm just going to give ye a quick hug and say see ye later!"

"You're welcome back anytime," Grace said hugging her.

Maisey gave a Hunter a look, then left for their rental car. He stepped forward and took Rebekah's hands in his. "I really am sorry I left you to deal with our parents alone. If it's any consolation, I honestly didn't believe they would actually disown you, but I should have known better. And I should have helped you when I found out."

"I appreciate that," Rebekah said through tears. "It's easy to blame you, but it isn't your fault. I could have gone back and continued to live the life they wanted me to, but I made the choice not to knowing full well what the consequences would be. It was you who gave me the courage to make that choice."

"Me?" he asked in surprise, "How?"

Rebekah shrugged. "You showed me what was possible by going out there and doing it first."

A huge grin spread across his face. "Thank you," he stated emphatically. "Now that you've forgiven me, I may actually be able to forgive myself." He looked between Rebekah and Grace. "It's still a little strange to see how close the two of you have become. From enemies to sisters in less than a year," he teased. "That can be the name of your Hallmark Movie!"

"Everything happens for a reason," Grace replied. "I'm going to pass on the movie, though, there's enough drama around here for at least a dozen movies. We don't need to add to the list."

"I don't want to say goodbye," he said sadly. "It feels so final. I know we need to live our lives, but I don't want this to be the last time I see you guys."

Grace gave him a last hug goodbye. "You know where to find us," she replied. "Just make sure to let us know you're coming next time," she teased.

"Scout's honor," he joked, giving them a mock salute.

"You were never in scout's," Rebekah rolled her eyes. "This guy," she said to Grace.

They all laughed and then he was gone. Which left Brianna, Maxwell, the boys, and Logan. Their goodbyes were nowhere near as emotional, which was a bit of a relief to Grace. She wasn't sure she could handle another round of tears, even if they were happy.

"Thank ye, Grace," Brianna said with a hug. "This was a special trip we'll never forget."

"It was lovely to meet you all," Grace replied. She high-fived the boys and gave a fist bump to Logan. Maxwell shook her hand, and then just like that, they were gone, leaving Rebekah and Grace alone.

"Any chance you want to put the cleaning off until tomorrow?" Rebekah asked hopefully.

Grace nodded enthusiastically. "I'm down with leaving it till Monday. This past week was exhausting!"

"Sounds good to me." She grabbed her purse and keys. "Thorne's supposed to move into his new house today so I'm going over to help out."

"Call me if you need help," Grace offered. "Otherwise, I'm going home to spend time with Cole and Granny."

Rebekah nodded and with a wave was gone. And then there was one, Grace thought. She gave one last look around, then headed out. What a difference a week can make.

***

Cole and Grace were snuggled up together on the couch. A fire crackled in the fireplace, as they talked softly so that only they could hear.

"It looks like Ruby and Piper had no problems adjusting to life here," Cole said with a nod toward the animals. Max and Ruby were passed out in their beds, while Piper lounged on Max's back.

"I think it helped that Max was here," said Grace. "They've always loved being around him."

He held her close, his arms wrapped around her back. "I don't suppose you've been by the house lately?" he asked. When Grace shook her head, he continued. "Jim is almost finished. In fact, he anticipates being done by the middle of next week."

"That's nice," Grace said absentmindedly. She listened to the beat of his heart as she laid there. If it were up to her, she'd spend the rest of her life just like this.

"Grace," he lifted her chin up with his forefinger so he could look in her eyes. "I don't want you to leave."

She furrowed her brow in confusion. "What do you mean? I'm not going anywhere."

"I don't mean now, silly, I mean ever. I don't want you to move back to Granny's. It's been so nice having you here. All of you. I didn't realize how lonely it is here until you moved in, and now...now I'm not sure I can handle things going back to the way they were."

Grace was still confused. They were supposed to get married in a couple of weeks, and then she would finally be able to officially move in with him. Was there something else going on? "Has something changed that I don't know about?"

"What do you mean?"

"I mean, why are you concerned about this? I thought we agreed I would move in here after the wedding?"

It was Cole's turn to look confused. "Did Molly forget to give you the message?"

"Um, what message?"

"Amelia sent you a tip," he explained. "It was for the same amount as the house repairs."

Grace sat up and stared at him in shock. "Are you serious?" When he nodded, she continued. "Amelia gave us a tip of fifteen thousand dollars? That's insane! Do you think it's a coincidence that the amount just happened to be enough to cover the repairs? Or do you think she found out somehow?"

"I have no idea," he replied. "But Grace, you're missing the point. Now that you have the money to cover the repairs, we don't have to move up our wedding."

"Says who?" she deadpanned. "I'm sorry Mr. Reed, but I am already attached to our new wedding date, and wild horses cannot make me change it. So you're just going to have to marry me as planned."

Cole reached over and pulled her back down to him. "I can live with that," he said softly. Her put his hand on the side of her face and gently tilted her head so he could kiss her. When he lifted his head, he stared into her eyes. "For the first time in my life, I'm actually looking forward to Christmas."

"It's going to be magical," Grace said, echoing Amelia's words.

"It already is."

Dear Reader,

Thank you so much for reading my book! Hunter's redemption has been a long time coming, and I am happy to finally see these characters get the closure they deserve.

I sincerely hope you enjoyed the scenes on Cole's farm. My husband grew up on a farm, and just like Granny and Gladys, his granny once fell in a mud hole trying to help out a cow. It was a funny story they like to tell, and I thought it would be amusing to add it to the book.

I'm looking forward to telling more stories set in Winterwood. There are more coming that feature Cole and Grace, as well as a spin-off series featuring new characters.

If you'd like with connect to me, I'm on Facebook at DiannaHouxShop, or you can find my author page on Amazon. You can also check out diannahouxshop.com

Happy Holidays!

-Dianna

About the Author

Hi! I'm a small-town girl who never outgrew her love for heartfelt stories and happily-ever-afters. I live in a rural Missouri town of twenty-five hundred people with my husband and three boys in a late 1800s home we're lovingly restoring—one project (and paintstroke) at a time.

When I'm not writing, I enjoy reading, perusing antique stores, or dreaming up my next story on the porch swing with glass of lemonade in hand!

My stories are seasoned with over-the-top, funny happenings in small-town settings, but at their heart, they're about real people with relatable struggles, hopes, and dreams. I write to entertain—and to remind readers that even the wildest moments can lead to something beautiful.

Learn more at diannahouxshop.com.

www.ingramcontent.com/pod-product-compliance
Lightning Source LLC
Chambersburg PA
CBHW022057050726
47591CB00002B/583